THE WHITE FLAG

The White Flag

MARCELLO VENTURI

translated from the Italian

by

WILLIAM CLOWES

New York

THE VANGUARD PRESS, INC.

Standard Book Number 8149-0004-6
Copyright, ©, mcmlxiv by Marcello Venturi
Translation coypright, ©, mcmlxvi by Anthony Blond Ltd.
Library of Congress Catalog Card Number: 70-79779

Manufactured in the United States of America

Translator's Note:

Cefalonia (Kephallinia: KEOHVAHNIA) lying to the west of Greece is the largest and southernmost island in the Ionian Archipelago. Thickly wooded and mountainous, its peaks rising to heights above five thousand feet afford magnificent views extending even to the mainland of the Peloponnese.

Its long and bloody history is familiar to classical scholars. Placed strategically at the opening of the bay of Lepanto and on the direct route from Greece to Italy, Reisland was subjected again and again in ancient times to war and invasion.

Early in the 13th century, when the power of Byzantium was declining, the island came under the domination of the Venetian Republic. In 1479 the islands in the Archipelago fell to the Turks, but were recaptured by Venice in 1500.

After 1797 when Napoleon had dissolved the Republic of Venice the French flag flew over Cefalonia, to be replaced by that of Britain in 1815. Not until 1863 were the Ionian Islands reunited with Greece.

The long association with Venice accounts for the Italianization of many place names in the island and for the architectural styles to be found there.

In the spring of 1941 after the defeat of Greece by the Axis Cefalonia was occupied by Italian troops. The garrison and the island's people lived peacefully, even happily, together until the armistice between the Badoglio Government of Italy and the Allies at the beginning of September 1943. In anticipation of this event the Germans had started to occupy the island.

After the armistice General Gandin, the commander of the

Acqui Division, units of which were at that time garrisoning the island, found himself in an unenviable dilemma: whether to obey the orders of Badoglio and resist the Germans or the orders of the Italian Command in Greece and surrender to the Germans.

He hesitated and his hesitation set in motion a chain of events which resulted in the slaughter of 341 officers and 4,750 men of the Acqui Division by the Germans.

The story told in this book is based on events recounted in the diary of Padre Luigi Ghilardini,* a chaplain with the division who survived the massacre, and on evidence given at the Court Martial in 1946–47 of several surviving officers of the division. In addition the author collected information from other survivors of the division, including Captain Amos Pampeloni, who opened fire on the Germans, and from eye-witnesses on Cefalonia.

* 'I Martiri di Cefalonia' Editrice Ligure.

PART ONE

CHAPTER ONE

1

I HAD CHOSEN the month of October because by then, even on an island in the Ionian Sea, the summer season is over and the holidaymakers have caught the boats back home. I did not feel like meeting a lot of tourists who did not belong to the island. I wanted to get to know the people who lived there and in particular Pasquale Lacerba, an Italian by birth, and by profession a photographer, and a woman named Katerina Pariotis. I wanted to see the island as it really was; as it must have been, or so I imagined, when Captain Aldo Puglisi, my father, had been there. I wanted to see the places where he had fought and the place where he had died.

A foreigner travelling so obviously outside the tourist season could not escape notice on the deck of the *Aghios Gerasimos*, the ferry which plied between Patras and the harbour of Sami, particularly as the boat was full of pilgrims and priests bound for the monastery of Aghios Erasmos, the patron saint of the island of Cefalonia.

Old peasant women in black dresses, with black scarves over their heads, had come aboard at Patras with wicker baskets and fibre suitcases. Throughout the voyage, huddled about the skirts and beards of their priests, they intoned mournful litanies in honour of the saint.

First the ship's captain and then an electrician from Athens had asked me whether I was a member of the orthodox church come over from Italy for the patron's festival. I had replied 'No' to both of them.

After that they had as good as asked me why I was going to Cefalonia and I had answered that I had some friends there,

Pasquale Lacerba the photographer and Katerina Pariotis. But neither of them had seemed to believe me.

I had shrugged my shoulders. It would have taken too long to explain it all to them. In fact, I knew no one on Cefalonia. If the truth were to be told I could not even claim to have known my father. I had no recollection of him at all. Had it not been for the photograph of him which stood on the chest of drawers in my mother's room, with a little lamp perpetually burning in front of it, I would not even have known what he looked like nor ever seen his smile sad with premonition.

The atmosphere of the big room where my parents had slept together into which I used to creep on tiptoe when my mother was out filled me with a feeling of fear and guilt. The big dark walnut wardrobe gave out a reassuring smell of well polished wood, but the double bed, empty behind me, seemed vast and menacing with its smooth blue bedspread which rose up to cover the mass of the twin pillows. For as long as I could remember my mother had slept there alone. I used to stand by the chest of drawers. In the half light that filtered through the heavy blinds aided by the feeble flame of the ever burning lamp, I would see my father's face come to life. His mouth would form itself into an expression of sadness and the grief in his eyes would become accentuated. It was as though he was saying that on the day when dressed in his smart artillery captain's uniform he had posed for a photograph to send to his wife, he had known that he was destined to die.

He had sent the photograph from Cefalonia. It was on a postcard and my mother used to say that it was not too bad a likeness although papa had been far more handsome. It was sepia tinted in the old fashioned manner, for as mother said with an indulgent shake of her head, what sort of a photographer would there have been on Cefalonia, a forgotten island at the end of the world?

The postcard was rather like blotting paper and on the back stamped in relief in roman characters was the photographer's name and address: Pasquale Lacerba, Via Principe di Piemonte 3, Argostoli.

10

A forgotten island, I thought to myself looking at the pale sea flecked with white by the rising wind, or at least an island off the track of the main shipping routes. To reach it I had had to disembark at Patras and board the ferry to the islands and this evening I would go ashore at Sami and then cross the Enos mountains by bus. Only then travelling through the darkness after a journey of two days and nights would I see the lights of Argostolion spread round the shores of the bay.

My mother had been right. I looked for the shape of the three islands that were somewhere in that part of the sea. I knew that Ithaca, Cefalonia and Zante were close together. I had seen them on the voyage to Patras, like dismasted hulks abandoned to drift on the waves. We had passed them in the distance and had left them dark with their pine forests floating in our wake. Of the three islands, Cefalonia is above all else associated with death. There was a time centuries ago when the island, unlike nowadays, had been a port of call for all the ships that crossed between Italy and Greece. In those days it went by the name of Epirus Nerus, Meloena or Teleboa and its position at the mouth of the bay of Lepanto subjected it to invasion and war. The first soldiers to land and to die on its beaches were Theban. Then came Athenians, the infantry of Philip of Macedonia, the legionaries of Rome, Normans, Venetians, Turks, and in more recent times French, Russians, and British from the Ionian garrisons.

I had first read of the island's history in a little red-covered book which my mother kept in a drawer amongst other mementoes; papers that meant nothing to me and which only she understood; yellow and white uniform buttons, a packet of dried-up *Three Star* cigarettes, love letters, field postcards, a diploma from the Ministry of Defence, and a silver commemorative medal. As well as Cefalonia's history I had learned the names of the principal towns that were marked on the map: Argostolion, Lixourion, San Giorgio di Castro and Sami, and the products of its valleys and hills, which were a little wheat, some fodder, currants and olives. I had learned too of the gentle character of the islanders, for the most part fishermen and peasants.

11

But neither geography books, nor a Touring Club guide issued in 1940, could give any information about the island's last invasion. On April 30, 1941, in the full light of midday, lumbering transport planes, 'Marsupials', appeared in the sky over Cefalonia, shattering the silence. They were accompanied by bombers and a swarm of tiny fighters circling round them like sheepdogs watching over their flocks. Hanging from great swaying umbrellas, Italian parachutists floated down to earth on the island. On their guard against attack from possible enemies they landed amongst the deserted vineyards, whilst the peasants watched them from their doorways.

Plainly neither the little red book nor the school textbooks could have told me any of this. I had learned it from other sources. Nor were they in a position to include a roll of the soldiers who were to lie buried in the forests of Cefalonia.

It was time now for someone to bring things up to date, I thought, as I tried to make out the island amongst the dark shadows which were visible behind the veil of autumn mist.

'Cefalonia', said the captain, stretching out his arm in front of him. Slowly the island drew near, materializing from out of the sea and the past.

Even though it was the same sea that my father had crossed in a troop transport escorted by warships, Cefalonia must have looked very different when he had first seen it. It would have been a day of sunshine and bright blue sea with the three islands standing high in the luminous spray. He and his artillerymen had no foreboding of death. The war against Greece was finished and won. Advancing into a conquered land he felt the flush of victory as the officers of the army of Thebes and of all the other armies that had landed there must have felt it. And now his name, Captain Aldo Puglisi, must be added to the list of those who in the course of centuries had died on Cefalonia.

Without any twilight to herald it, night had fallen suddenly. The island stretched before us in a wall of darkness pierced here and there by the faint lights of Sami. On board the ferry the lights were turned on, too. The pilgrims and their priests crowded the ship's rails, gazing in silence at the island as though they were frightened of it. From the forests, now close by, a humid wind carried the smell of wet leaves and earth on to the decks of the *Aghios Gerasimos*.

2

'Yes, you are right, I am an Italian and I am looking for a fellow countryman. He is called Pasquale Lacerba. He is a photographer and lives at Number 3, Via Principe di Piemonte, in Argostolion.'

'Principe di what?'

'Oh, I am sorry. I do not suppose that it is called that any more. Principe di Piemonte was its name during the war.'

'Probably it is called Via Principe Constantinos now. I live in Argostolion but I can never remember the names of the streets; and me a taxi driver!'

'Ah well, just the same things happen to me in my town at home.'

'Where do you come from, if I am not being nosey?'

'Milan.'

'And if I have understood you aright, you were looking for a photographer.'

'A photographer called Pasquale Lacerba.'

'Pasquale Lacerba. I have a feeling I know the name.'

'Via Principe Constantinos, Number 3.'

'If the earthquake did not kill him off, of course. When did you see him last?'

'Well, to tell you the truth, I have never seen him at all.'

'Never seen him?'

'No, never.'

'Well then, it may be he really did die in the earthquake.'

'I am also looking for a woman named Katerina Pariotis.'

'Katerina who?'

'Katerina Pariotis.'

'No, never heard of her. Can you tell me what she looks like, or haven't you seen her either?'

'No, never.'

'I see. I expect you are bringing them messages from relations in Italy, aren't you?'

'Yes, that's it; more or less.'

'That's what I thought. This Katerina Pariotis, is she Greek or Italian? Or, perhaps she's an Italian married to a Greek?'

'I really don't know.'

'I hope you have got good news for them, if they are still alive.'

'Oh, yes, quite good.'

'I am glad to hear it. Now tell me, do you think I speak Italian well?'

'Very well, I should say.'

'My name is Sandrino. If ever you want me, you can find me down at the harbour.'

'Right, Sandrino.'

'I have got a taxi, a Studebaker, if you want to see the island. In the mornings and evenings I drive this bus from Argostolion to Sami and back, but the rest of the day I am a taxi driver. You can always find me at the harbour or in the market or in Piazza Valianos. Ask for me, ask for Sandrino, if you want to see the island in a Studebaker. It won't cost you a lot.'

'I will certainly ask for Sandrino.'

'For 300 drachmae, I'll show you Cefalonia from top to bottom.'

'Tell me one thing.'

'What is it, Signore?'

'Are you a Greek?'

'I knew you would ask me that. I'm half and half; half Greek, half Italian. Twenty years ago I was a fisherman in Sicily and then I ended up here.'

We had to shout to be heard, because the pilgrims and the priests who had boarded the bus too had started to sing again. It was a small bus; just a tin box on wheels. The windows were open to the night and through them came a wind which fluttered the discoloured blinds, but there was still a smell of robes and beards. To the singing of the pilgrims was added the noise of the engine which boiled from the exertion of climbing the hills, the groaning of the springs, and the screech of the tires on the road. I was sitting in front almost on top of the driver in order not to be swamped by the black, chanting mass of women. In the yellow light of the headlamps I saw that we were passing through mountains. There were olive trees to the left of the road and on the right the drop of a precipice, the parapet of a bridge, and milestones. We were climbing up towards the sky once more clear and full of stars that rocked across the windscreen. When I turned my head, I saw the open mouths of the pilgrims showing pink amidst the black of their headscarves.

I looked out, peering into the darkness. This was the road which my father must have taken with his battery to reach Argostolion. They would have been in a convoy of trucks, with their lights dimmed, with these same olive trees at the roadside, the same bridges even, and the same milestones. If I put my head by the window I was breathing the same night air of Cefalonia that he would have breathed. It was air heavy with the fragrance of the woods, the smell of the earth blended with the subtle softness of the sea whose presence was still with us though it was now far behind.

At the summit of the pass the bus stopped. In a babble of sound the pilgrims and the priests got down with their baskets and suitcases. Robes fluttered through the light of the headlamps like birds' wings and disappeared towards the dark bulk of the monastery. The bus was now almost empty with only a couple of young men in the back seat looking like peasants dressed for a festa. We set off down hill, freewheeling at breakneck speed, our bonnet pointing towards the lights of Argostolion which disappeared and reappeared at every bend. The lights came closer and grew bigger. Soon I could make out the bridge of whose existence I had heard. It spanned the bay; a long streak of dark masonry flung across the mirror of the sea. The town itself was invisible behind a wall of street lamps. Along the coast, every light seemed to be burning and reflected in the motionless water. As we moved towards the centre, all I could succeed in seeing of the outskirts were a few isolated lamps. Seen from the bus Argostolion seemed to be one long row of single storey houses facing the sea.

It was not a very impressive sight. From talk I had heard and from pictures in books, I had expected something quite different. Nonetheless, although I was not admitting it I felt strangely moved.

'Remember my name, Sandrino,' the driver said once more with a wink.

3

Viewed in the clean washed light of morning, the impression was even worse than in the evening when I had got down from the bus. I had read about the earthquake of 1953 in the papers, but I had never imagined that the devastation was anything like this. As I looked incredulously out of my window in the Hotel Enos, Argostolion was there before me like the bones of some dead carcass on a mountainside. There were no tiled roofs to create that diversity of levels that typifies a town. There was not a single large building around Piazza Valianos. On three sides it was lined with low non-descript buildings, newly plastered and painted, with flat grey slabs for roofs instead of tiles. The fourth side opposite the hotel was empty and gave on to the hillside where market gardens with walls of broken stone, paths worn by the rain, and the remains of an old asphalt road without footwalks or houses were visible. A pale sun feeble from a night of rain struggled against the clouds.

I went out into the piazza and walked past the wooden benches which stood amongst the flower beds beneath palm trees bent in the wind. I was looking in amazement for some sign of Argostolion as it had been. Perhaps the four trees, or those old fashioned gas lamps weathered by time and now festooned with electric bulbs, or perhaps the dark green bronze statue of a man seated on a stool gazing into space, had always been here. But everything else, all the old town, what had happened to it? And its inhabitants, had they disappeared too and with them Pasquale Lacerba and Katerina Pariotis? I walked slowly along the pavement which surrounded the piazza on three sides and then sat down at a table under a canopy outside the first café that I came to. I was doubtful if any waiter would come to take my order.

With growing anxiety I wondered what would have happened to the points of reference that I had gathered together with such care over so many years. Apart from Pasquale Lacerba and Katerina Pariotis the only clues I had were geographical and I had followed them up in school books and the Touring Club guide. I had found the names of places in the letters to my mother, in an account of what had happened written by two army chaplains who had escaped and in the garbled memoirs of one or two other survivors.

There was the Casetta Rossa where my father and hundreds of other officers had been shot and the road to Capo San Teodoro. I knew that the road ran out of the town to the left and ran along the edge of the bay, past the sea wells and sea mills and reached the bend by the Casetta opposite the open sea and a little lighthouse on the rocks. But would the Casetta and the road and the lighthouse and all the rest still be there? I wondered as I looked at the nonexistent town on the hill.

The waiter stood beside me. He was a little man with a wispy fair moustache, a round face with pinkish, mouselike eyes which were fixed on me attentively. He had not put on his white coat, but was in his shirt sleeves with his hairy arms bare.

'Coffee', I said.

'Italian?' he asked, his moustache twitching on his lip like a mouse's whiskers.

I gave a sigh of relief. Argostolion was inhabited after all. We looked at each other with interest. At a rough guess he was about fifty. He might well have been a waiter before the earthquake and even during the occupation.

'Me like Italians,' he said smiling. Motionless, he went on looking at me, a dirty rag in his hand and a cigarette stuck behind his ear like our waiters at home in a tavern.

'Me know Italians,' he went on, and after a pause added 'Italians good, Germans bad.'

He went back into the café and came out with a small cup of Turkish coffee and a glass of cloudy water on a yellow zinc tray. Still smiling, still looking at me closely, he put the tray down on the table. It seemed to me that it was as though he wanted to recognize in me the face of someone else, someone he had know in days gone by.

'Shall I ask him? Will he remember?' I wondered.

We started to talk about the earthquake and the island. No, he told me, not all the Cefaliots had died. A few people had been killed but for the most part they had been civil servants from Patras. The Cefaliots, peasants, fishermen, shopkeepers were used to earthquakes. The moment the island had given a tremble, they had rushed out into the open, to the fields and hills, and had saved themselves.

'Only clerks from Patras,' he repeated with a grin. He took the cigarette from behind his ear and lit it.

'And Pasquale Lacerba, the photographer, did he escape too?' I asked him. 'Also him,' the waiter answered without hesitation and added with an air of doing me a favour, 'Pasquale Lacerba, he my friend.'

'And Katerina Pariotis?' The little man wrinkled his forehead. 'The schoolmistress, Katerina Pariotis?' I urged him.

No, he knew nothing of her. She was not a customer of his café. But he was sure that she would have escaped, too.

I would have liked to have asked him if, amongst the Italian officers, he had known a Captain Aldo Puglisi, a good deal like me in looks, but taller, but I lacked the courage. It would be easier to ask Pasquale Lacerba, who, because I had thought about him so much, seemed almost like a relation.

I drank coffee, took a sip of water and rose to my feet.

'Salut,' the waiter said, shaking me by the hand.

CHAPTER TWO

1

PASQUALE LACERBA was sitting in front of the counter. His legs were stuck out across the floor and his stick leant against his chair back. Beneath his nose was an open paper. He raised his head and looked at me in silence over his glasses with dark, burning southern eyes.

We stared at each other without speaking. I felt embarrassed standing in front of that pale, bony face and those long, stretched out legs.

The shop was like a sort of well with Pasquale Lacerba seated at the bottom, his back against a hardboard partition. His legs crossed the floor from side to side, blocking my path. Rapidly I glanced at the walls. They were higher than they were wide and were covered all round the room with picture postcards of Cefalonia. There were photographs of the countryside, houses, valleys, mountains and beaches, and above them were hanging pictures of saints. Many of them were coloured and fixed in ornate tin frames or painted like icons. They all had long white beards and wide open eyes, staring away into the distance.

'Pasquale Lacerba?' I said softly.

With difficulty he stood up on his long twisted legs. He put the paper on the counter and leant on his stick which he had taken from the back of the chair. He looked at me carefully through his spectacles and once again I had the feeling that he, like the waiter, might be looking for someone else as he studied my features. 'I am the son of Captain Puglisi; Aldo Puglisi of the 33rd Regiment of Artillery,' I said rather foolishly, trying to jog his memory.

Pasquale Lacerba's face became more tense, and the skin over his bony cheeks more yellow and more drawn. The dark fire in his eyes took on a reddish tinge.

'Italian,' he said.

He stretched out his hand and I took it in mine. It was as dry as a piece of wood. He pointed to the empty chair and leant against the partition.

'Sit down,' he said. 'Did you have a good journey?'

I sat down beneath the icons and the postcards. Saints of the Orthodox Church gazed down at me from every angle.

'Do you like them?' asked Pasquale Lacerba, as he followed my gaze.

'Who are they?' I replied, just for something to say.

His loose jacket flapping, he hovered over me like a great captive bird, dark against the light from the glass door, and pointed with his stick at the walls. He told me their names one by one: Aghios Nicolaos, Aghios Spiridione, Aghios Gerasimos, and so on.

'I do not paint them,' he explained lowering his stick. 'I take photographs. An Italian friend in Athens sends them to me and I sell them to the tourists.'

He fetched another chair from behind the counter and sat down facing me with his hands folded on the handle of his stick. 'I will sell you some cheap,' he said looking at me. 'How much?' I asked. 'They're usually forty drachmae,' he answered, 'but for Italian tourists they are thirty.'

'I will buy one before I leave.'

'They're fine mementoes of Cefalonia. What part of Italy are you from?'

He gave me no time to reply. He was originally from Bari, he told me, and had lived on the island for years; he could not even remember how long. It was a lovely island. It was a pity I had come at that time of the year, right at the beginning of the rainy season, otherwise I could have gone to see the beach at Nassos, bathed there and made a trip up Enos and to the fortress of San Giorgio.

He fell silent as the strangeness of my visit, out of season, struck him. I saw him look surprised. 'Why have you come so late?' he asked. Then at last I was able to tell him that I was not interested in being a tourist. I had come to Cefalonia to see where my father had died, to see the Casetta Rossa and all the other places, and that I was looking for Katerina Pariotis, the primary schoolteacher.

Bent over his stick with his chin resting on his hands and his eyes fixed on his shoes, he listened to me in silence. He sat completely still, apparently intent on my words; so still that I began to doubt if he really was listening to me.

'Are you listening to me?' I asked eventually. But Pasquale Lacerba had not replied. He went on staring at his shoes as though he had completely forgotten my presence.

'No,' he said, 'I don't remember,' and after a pause he added as though to justify himself, 'how could I remember everything?'

He got up suddenly with a brusque gesture of his hand as though he wanted to push away his recollections.

The pearl-like light, both clear and opaque at the same time, foretold more rain. 'You've chosen the wrong time of year,' Pasquale said again, looking at the sky with disgust. 'But see,' he went on, moving behind the counter and opening a box, 'Cefalonia really can be beautiful.'

He spread out a packet of photographs on the wooden surface. I rose to my feet and picked one up at random. Pasquale watched eagerly to see my surprise.

There was a view of the city as it had been before the earthquake, with houses and streets climbing up the side of the hill right to the crest. Another photograph showed the seafront crowded with people, a cargo boat moored to the quay and caiques with their sails reflected in the waters of the bay. Others showed a mountain top covered with pines and spruces standing out against the light of morning and the monastery of Aghios Gerasimos in the valley below.

'You see?' said the photographer.

'Lovely,' I said, 'You are a real artist and a fine photographer.'

'You like them?' he asked, his cunning eyes studying me carefully. 'If they're any use to you you can have them cheap.'

'I will take some home as a souvenir,' I said.

'And some icons as well?'

'Yes,' I replied, 'I will get them before I go.'

Satisfied, he put them away in a drawer and came back into the middle of the shop in which there was hardly room for us both and our cigarette smoke.

'Before the war and the earthquake, it must have been really beautiful here,' I said, to pick up the thread of our conversation. 'And have you always been a photographer, even during the occupation?'

Pasquale smiled. 'I was born between the lens and the plate,' he answered. 'My father was a photographer before me. He worked around Bari with his tripod on his back and me behind him learning the trade. He took photographs at religious festivals, weddings, first communions. He even took the dead. I can see them now, stretched out on their beds in their Sunday clothes with their hands crossed. They terrified me and gave me nightmares.' But I returned to the point and said, 'And during the occupation?' Pasquale fell silent and for a moment we remained without speaking: I, trying to find some friendly expressions of encouragement, he, trying to make out what I was after.

'I was an interpreter,' he said. 'I had no choice. There I was, the only person on Cefalonia who could speak Italian. What would you have done in my place?' 'I would have become an interpreter,' I replied. 'You see?' Pasquale threw open his arms as though to emphasize the inescapability of destiny. 'When the war was over,' he went on with indignation, 'the Andartes descended on the town and arrested me, but the Cefaliots, who had always wished well of me and still do, protested, and so they were forced to leave me in peace.' Now he was speaking quietly in a flat voice and once again became lost in his memories. But only for a moment and then he made a quick gesture through the air blue with smoke and said that he had enough of the war and that it was better to talk of something else.

'But now I am Greek,' he said, 'and I married a Greek wife.'

'Have you had some coffee?' he asked me. We went out

22

and bending against the wind made our way towards Piazza Valianos.

We walked between two rows of shabby little shops on a footpath of beaten earth softened by rain. In the middle of the road the storm water had washed an olive branch and a clump of grass on to a stone during the night's downpour. In spite of the wind it was not cold. The air was sweet and smelt of the sea.

'If the wind keeps on like this,' Pasquale said, holding on to his battered old grey hat, ' the ferry from Patras won't be able to run.'

At the foot of the streets which ran down to the sea front we could see that the waters of the bay were whipped to a fury. The waves were rolling in and breaking over the bridge. All along the shore the sea was pounding up beyond the beaches on to the grassy slopes behind them.

Pasquale stopped and wedging his stick in a crack in the road pointed down towards the bay. 'You see the bridge? It is the only structure that escaped the earthquake.'

I was thinking anxiously about the ferry which might have to interrupt its service between Sami and Patras because beyond the mouth of the bay out in the open, the sea would be even rougher than it was here. The slender thread which joined the island to the mainland might be broken and for a day, a week, perhaps even for a year Cefalonia would be completely cut off.

'Let's go to Nicolino's,' the photographer said, and he limped off between the flowerbeds and benches in the piazza as though the sight of the café tables had given him a new lease of life. In the corner of the piazza two taxis, great American cars, long and highly coloured, were standing. From a window of one a head and a hand hung out. I recognized them as Sandrino's. He shouted a greeting to me. 'Can I take you anywhere?' he asked. He got out and came with us to the café. All three of us sat down at a table sheltered from the wind.

'Let's have some ouzo, too,' suggested Pasquale. He made clear to Sandrino that he was not wanted and that he was wasting his time. But the taxi-driver went on repeating that for a few drachmae he would take me all round the island and show me all the sights. He had, so he said, already been to Sami that morning to meet the ferry and had seen it set sail back to Patras in spite of the rough seas.

'Shall we go and see the fortress?' he asked, looking first at me and then at the photographer. Pasquale showed his displeasure by gazing over Sandrino's head with his jaws clenched without replying, as though he could neither see nor hear him. I wanted to get a little more out of the photographer before I started exploring the island and so I put Sandrino off with 'tomorrow or this afternoon'.

'Fine, I shall be there,' he said, indicating his huge yellow and red car. 'And what about Katerina Pariotis?' he called out to me from the middle of the square. I shrugged my shoulder. 'I'll look for her for you,' he cried. Pasquale smiled and made a face.

We drank the ouzo. It was a sort of absinthe, very strong and clear as crystal when neat, but the addition of even a drop of water turned it dense and cloudy in the glass. It gave off an aroma of wild grasses and flowers.

'When the Germans landed,' I asked him point blank, watching the cloud of ouzo in my glass, 'what happened on the island? How did the Italian soldiers react? Was there any feeling of smouldering hostility or were relations between the Germans and the Italians quite normal?' Pasquale looked at me in surprise. 'Nothing happened,' he answered. 'The Germans and the Italians were still allies. I don't remember that anything happened.'

2

'Oh, yes,' he added, as if his mind had at last pierced the haze of time. 'There was a lot of movement amongst the troops. For instance, I remember that an Italian battery was sent to support a German infantry unit at Lixourion. They were good friends. The officers ate together every evening; Italians and Germans sitting together at the same table.

'Have some more ouzo,' I said to him in order to encourage his reminiscences.

'Willingly,' he replied.

The wind had fallen and the clouds which were still being blown across the mountain tops showed gaps of blue from time to time, and now and then a ray of sunlight lit first one corner of the piazza and then another.

'Until the armistice,' he went on, 'nothing happened except the movement of troops. No one could have foreseen what was soon to take place. Who could have imagined it?' he whispered, looking at me, but as though talking to himself.

'They walked down the streets together,' he said, pointing with his stick towards the piazza, still strangely deserted and without traffic, 'and all the time they ate at the same table.'

It still surprised him, even now. But at this distance in time he could ask the question without fear, just from curiosity, whilst he concentrated his attention on the reality of the glass of ouzo.

3

We walked down the tree lined avenue leaving Piazza Valianos behind us. Pasquale was limping along leaning on his stick, but he had not wanted us to take Sandrino's taxi. Gradually we left the town behind us. The avenue turned into a lane with the sea almost washing it to the right and the slope of the mountain thick with pines on the left. Pasquale talked on and on jumping from one subject to another. Maybe it was this inability to stick to the point that caused my depression, and his wide flapping trousers that seemed empty, his torn lapels and his jacket, an indefinable colour, grey with something of yellow in it, as though time itself had given it a patina.

'I will take you there, to Katerina Pariotis' house,' he had said. I knew we were taking the route to San Teodoro, the path of the last journey that my father had made before he was shot; but Pasquale Lacerba was disturbing my thoughts by telling me a story about some friend of his in Patras who followed some obscure trade. Then he started to talk about the feast of Aghios Gerasimos which had started that day at the monastery, and said that if the weather remained fine as it promised to do, we would be able to go up there to see the procession.

I interrupted him to ask if the Casetta Rossa was not some-where near where we were and he broke off his discourse to say that it was near by.

It was this way that the trucks had passed laden with the officers and men of the Acqui Division who were being taken to be shot. My father had been in one of those trucks. He must have seen those same trees for the earthquake had not succeeded in destroying them, the same outline of mountains and the same sea coming in between the rocks and bushes. As we went on and as the trucks must have gone on, the smell of the sea became stronger as the two arms of the bay spread out and the open sea stretched before us. The little tower of the lighthouse came into view and behind it the Mediterranean in all its vastness.

They had seen all this on their last journey, just as we were seeing it now, except that the sea might have been calmer, almost motionless in the clear light of morning – it had all started in the morning – not flecked with white, with the waves still running even though the wind had dropped. It had been a still, breathless day with the silence broken only by the coming and going of the trucks which went back and forth from Capo San Teodoro each time with a fresh load of prisoners. From time to time the peace of the day had been shattered by bursts of machine gun fire coming from the direc-tion of the Casetta Rossa.

In front of us, standing a little way back from the shore, four grey stone walls stood in ruins. Pasquale explained to me that they were the remains of a sea mill. Before the earth-quake there had been a number of them here and there along the coast. They were worked by the sea which poured with the force of a torrent inside a sort of well. These sea wells, he went on, pointing with his stick at a hole in the ground carved through the porous rock at the bottom of which the sea bubbled, were joined together by unexplained subterranean channels.

'It is not known,' said Pasquale almost awed by the mystery which surrounded him, 'how the water gets from the sea. Geologists have come from all over the world to study the phenomenon without finding the answer and they have gone home empty handed.'

We walked on again. Beneath the pine trees which came down to the edge of the road stretched garden walls, covered with grass and moss. They were almost intact but in their midst there stood only the ruins of houses. This must have been the most elegant part of the island where the villas were. I could picture them all rose red and blue with green shutters through which the curtains of the rooms could be seen, or a bedhead, or a lampshade. Now the enclosures were empty except for rubble and undergrowth. Beside some of the walls there were wooden huts, little houses in miniature, painted pink with blue doors and windows and green shutters.

'Here we are,' said Pasquale Lacerba, stopping at a rusty iron gate. Steps of broken stone led up to one of these little houses. An iron lamp hung in the porch on both sides of which were small beds of flowers whose scent filled the roadway. Behind the house was a stretch of overgrown garden ending in the wood.

It was here that my father used to come to sleep, not in this very house, but he must have stopped his motor-cycle about here on the road. Perhaps these steps were there then. On his journey in the back of the truck he must have turned his head about here in the hope of catching a last glimpse through the closed shutters of Katerina Pariotis, her parents and the little room that he had rented.

We went up the steps, the photographer going first, his stick tapping on the stones and his stiff right leg dragging painfully behind him.

We stood in the porch under the lamp which looked as

27

though it had come from a ship. Pasquale Lacerba knocked on the plywood door with the carved handle of his stick. We heard the sound of footsteps. The door opened and in the rectangle of shadow appeared the face of Katerina Pariotis, pale and thin in the clear light of morning. Her hair was streaked with grey and she looked a little untidy.

Pasquale Lacerba spoke to her and was evidently explaining who I was and why we had come looking for her. As he went on talking she gazed at my face as if, and this time I was certain that I was not mistaken, as if she recognized in me the face of my father. I smiled at her, embarrassed by a sudden feeling of guilt.

I wondered why I had come to awaken these people's memories. Only then beneath Katerina's gaze did I realize that I was taking unfair advantage of them. I was violating their recollections, forcing my way into their past and by my presence making them remember things that they had long since forgotten.

'Come in,' said Katerina. Her voice struck a contrast to her rather jaded face. It was fresh and beautiful, the voice of a girl. 'Come in,' she said, but we could not because she just stood in the doorway looking at me.

'Why don't you come in?' Katerina Pariotis said at last, moving out of the doorway. She smiled and her smile, too, was young and fresh like her voice. We went in, Pasquale Lacerba preceding me and talking in Greek about something I did not understand.

CHAPTER THREE

1

THE LIVINGROOM was just like many of ours at home in Italian country houses. We sat on a sofa covered in red velvet. There was a vase of flowers on a table in the middle of the room. On the wooden walls – the whole house was of wood, prefabricated from material supplied by the Swedish Red Cross – some photographs hung. There was the face of an old moustached peasant in his best clothes with his shirt buttoned to the neck but without a tie, and an old woman with the folds of a black headscarf falling to her shoulders, her wide open eyes fixed on the camera lens. An electric lamp with a glass shade hung by a short wire from the ceiling. Beyond the table a sideboard occupied the whole of a wall. On the top, as there would have been at home, there were more photographs of saints, weddings, first communions, and so on, with coloured postcards of cities and harbours, amongst which was one of a steamship under way, with the sea curling back from its bow.

A door opened and a man in shirt sleeves came into the room.

'This is my husband,' said Katerina Pariotis.

'Italian?' he asked. 'I speak, a little.'

He had a fine bronzed face with blue eyes, transparent as glass. He told me that he knew Italy, La Spezia, Brindisi, Genoa, Naples, and then even before I had inquired I recognized him as a sailor. 'Yes,' he said, 'sailor. Retired now, all finished.'

He pointed to the postcard of the ship. It had been his, he explained, the *Egnatia*. His blue eyes lit up and a smile played across his lips, as though he was speaking of a son.

'Can I offer you some coffee?' he asked. 'It is all ready on the stove.'

'Yes, please,' replied Pasquale.

I said I did not want any. I was tired of drinking Turkish coffee, but the retired sea-captain put his hand on my shoulder and patted it affectionately, as though to make me change my mind. He had a hand like the sail of a windmill, huge and strong, covered with weatherbeaten skin. 'Coffee, coffee,' he said.

He took a tin of biscuits from the sideboard and thrust it at me and at Pasquale, who took a handful. I took one, though I really did not feel hungry.

Katerina Pariotis came into the room and put a zinc tray down on the table. On it there were four cups of steaming coffee and the same number of glasses of water. When she sat down in a wicker chair by the window which gave on to the wood I could see her profile. I wondered whether, living in the same house, she and my father had been lovers. It was certainly a possibility. I looked at her out of the corner of my eye while I listened to the voice of the old sailor. She still had a certain faded beauty, notwithstanding the lines on her face and the grey streaks in her hair. Her husband was telling a story about exotic places in the Lebanon or somewhere like that, but I was only listening with half my attention. With the other half I was intent on Katerina as she sipped her cup of coffee. She had long, thin hands which made the cup seem even smaller than it really was. If she realized that I was looking at her, she certainly did not show it, though suddenly she gave me a long glance which took me in from head to foot, from my muddy shoes to my hair. Her eyes passed over me and then beyond me, but did not miss one detail of me. I felt as though she had seen even what lay inside me.

The sailor and Pasquale were discussing me and why I had come to see Katerina Pariotis, in Greek. Amidst the flow of incomprehensible words I heard my father's name, Aldo Puglisi, again and again. The sailor's face became thoughtful and then distressed. He looked at me with pity.

'Gesu!' I thought, 'what can Pasquale Lacerba be telling him? He is going to make him weep.'

Katerina collected up the cups and left the room. I heard her at the sink, washing them up. She came back only when Pasquale had finished his tale and said something to him in Greek which again I did not understand.

I felt myself an outsider caught in a trap. I would have liked to run away. Why ever, I asked myself, had I come to unbury the past?

'Your father – dead here,' said the old sea captain, and indicating his wife he added, 'Katerina knows.'

And now I felt afraid. I would have liked to have said 'Let's talk about your ship. Let's talk about Italy. Tell me, captain, were you ever in Milan?' But Katerina's eyes pinned me to the sofa and prevented me from speaking.

2

But she was not recalling the scene of his death. She was thinking of the sequel to the night by the sea mills. She did not remember exactly what day it was, whether it was Aghios Christoforos or Aghios Nicolaos, but it was one of the afternoons when the two of them had been together amongst the rocks near the lighthouse.

3

I did not know what to make of her long silence, as she stood in the doorway of the kitchen. Her husband stood beside her waiting too, while the photographer munched biscuits fished from the bottom of his cup with a spoon.

'Katerina knows,' her husband said, as though he wanted to recall her to the present and to remind her of the presence of himself, of Pasquale Lacerba, and of me, the son of the dead man.

She smiled wistfully. Her eyes were deep and tired.

'He came during the night,' she said. 'I heard a knocking on the door and I ran to open it. Down there at San Teodoro the fires were burning.'

CHAPTER FOUR

1

As KATERINA talked she looked in front of her, but she was seeing things from the past which I had invoked and could not now succeed in driving back. It was clear that she was not telling all she knew.

She tried to speak unemotionally in her usual voice, but her accents of grief did not escape me. Memory lit fires in her eyes and her voice sounded now soft now deep like light and shade in a valley.

'Captain Aldo Puglisi died,' she said at the conclusion of her story, still looking in front of her, 'with your mother's name on his lips.'

I saw him breathing his last on Katerina's bed; his face bloodstained, his chest bare and his head high on the pillows. But I could not hear my mother's name. And why then did Katrina lower her eyes and avoid mine?

All the time I had been listening to her I had been thinking of what she must have been like as a girl, twenty years before. Her expression and her voice convinced me more and more that there had been something between the two of them.

The idea did not disturb me. Not because I had any resentment towards my mother, who had brought me up and nourished me on the cult of my father's memory, or because of any sudden feeling for Katerina, but because the idea of an affair between this woman and my father would help me to clothe a legend with flesh and blood and make him real.

I had been born and grown up with the heroic legend of a father who had died standing up against the wall of a house crying 'Viva l'Italia!' The legend included Cefalonia, an island

33

far from the world, vague and unreal like all islands and all legendary things. According to my mother's stories he had been an exemplary father and officer. So exemplary, that I had never really been able to see his face. It had always been a little blurred and deprived of substance and reality. Only now, here in this wooden walled living room in the presence of Katerina in slippers and dressing-gown, with the old sailor at my side and Pasquale Lacerba slouched in a chair munching biscuits, only now did I begin to see my father, amongst things and people existing on this island, real and solid, remote though it was. At the suggestion of her husband and Pasquale Lacerba Katerina had brought in three glasses of ouzo and some water, and as I looked at her a troubling thought came to me; she had meant more to my father than had my mother. She had been the real woman in his life.

I took my glass of ouzo and added water to it. It was my second or third that morning, I did not remember exactly.

Pasquale Lacerba had started to talk about the war. Now and again Katerina interrupted or corrected him while she went in and out of the kitchen or sat down uneasily. The old sailor joined in from time to time.

I did not understand much of what they were saying. They seemed to have forgotten my existence. They spoke in Greek, talking of the armistice.

2

'All that Colonel Barge had at his command were three thousand grenadiers of 996th Regiment, no more,' said Pasquale Lacerba. 'This was the full strength of the German garrison at the time of the armistice.

'If the Italians had only taken the initiative, then and there,' he went on, looking at me and pointing at me, an Italian, with a biscuit held between his thumb and index finger, 'the whole thing would have turned out quite differently.' He glared at me as though the blame for what had happened was mine.

'And what about the German aeroplanes?' I asked. They were something I had read about in some book of memoirs and I wanted to know what had happened. But Pasquale shrugged his shoulders as though to say, nonsense! He ate his last biscuit staring at the floor.

'Even today we do not really know,' said Katerina Pariotis. She was talking to Pasquale, not to me, but she spoke in a quiet resigned voice in Italian so that I, too, would understand.

'No one,' she said, 'can change the path of fate.'

It was plain that she was trying to spare me any embarrassment from Pasquale's outspoken words, but I did not feel embarrassed, rather humbled. The old sailor seemed to want to comfort me too and he patted me on the back, passing me the tin of biscuits. 'Take one,' he said.

'But the Germans,' Pasquale went on, 'yes, they could have been stopped; three thousand Germans.' He got up and moved restlessly between the table and the sofa, leaning on his stick, looking out of the two windows, now at the wood and now at the road and the bay, as though the little room was too small to contain his feelings. 'The Germans were the hand of fate,' said Katerina conciliatorily.

CHAPTER FIVE

1

THE ROAD to Capo San Teodoro turned to the left and ran along the edge of the wood. The wind had dropped completely by now and the sea was calmer. A ray of warm sunlight playing here and there on the surface of the bay traced a pattern across it.

Pasquale Lacerba said that the weather would now remain fine. I had been worrying about the ferry and thought with relief that the slender life line that united us with Patras and the rest of the world would not be broken.

'We have a very fine festa at Aghios Gerasimos monastery,' Pasquale said once more. 'If local customs interest you, we can go up there this afternoon on the bus. We could get some good photographs.'

We arrived at the Casetta Rossa, or rather at what would once have been its garden. It was to our right where the road curved.

The road went on to the left towards the extreme point of the island. Here at the bend, the roadway bordered on a meadow which ran to the foot of a ruined wall, not more than half a yard high, built of earth and stones weathered by the rain. Beyond the wall lay the open sea, but to reach it a stretch of white stones, sea wells and rocks would have had to be crossed. At each of the crumbled ends of the walls, there stood the rotten trunk of a tamarisk. They seemed to be there specially to frame the view, and it may be that for this reason the owners of the house had planted them.

We left the road and walked across the yielding carpet of

36

camp, tangled grass and mud. We had gone straight up to the wall and stood there looking at the sea and the distant horizon. The last horizon that he and they had seen. I turned to look at the ruins of the house. Like the rest of Cefalonia, the Casetta had ceased to exist. But here, no one, not even the old owners, had come back to rebuild it, if only as a prefabricated wooden hut.

The garden, now a field, was quite deserted. The house was a pile of stones and bricks, broken steps and pieces of wall still intact but bleached by the weather. Here lay a shutter, there a rusty hinge, a piece of blackened tile and a door latch. Over the ruins and the traces of the foundations grew weeds and nettles. Bougainvillea climbed over piles of earth and clumps of big aloes gave out their heavy scent.

Here, against the wall, they were shot. If they had had their backs to the wall, without doubt they would have seen this stretch of sea and horizon framed by the two tamarisk trees. It was morning when the shooting started, a fine September morning. If, on the other hand, they were shot in the back, then their eyes must have rested on this wall now reduced to ruins and on these pieces of rubble and stone green with age that had comprised it.

I left the wall and wandered among the ruins. From out of the earth amidst clumps of wild grass protruded a rotting shoe, a yellow comb, the remains of a bathing dress, a bottle, a cardboard box with some English printing on it. From the other side of the garden Pasquale Lacerba watched me sadly. They were not things from that time, he explained. It was useless to look for any trace of the executions there. Before they had left the island the Germans had taken great pains to cover their traces. They had burnt or buried everything.

At his words I retraced my steps and left the ruins, because I realized that it upset him to see me searching amongst the rubble. It was as if I were searching for something that was inside him, rummaging about in his innards. His face looked drawn. He stood there on the grass, thin and pale, leaning on his stick.

I went towards him. Behind the lenses of his glasses his eyes looked frightened. But it was not at me that he was looking, nor at the ruins of the Casetta Rossa. He was not gazing at anything that was there.

CHAPTER SIX

1

WE RETURNED slowly towards Argostolion. Pasquale Lacerba seemed quite calm as he walked beside me. He was limping along almost happy now that we had left the garden of the Casetta Rossa behind us. Life, his thin, worn, pale face seemed to say, was going on despite everything; despite natural and unnatural death at the hands of man or of nature.

We came up the short avenue of eucalyptus which ended in Piazza Valianos. Its surface was broken and cracked. Washed clean by the rain, the trees shone. At the end of this green avenue the piazza bathed in sunshine seemed even more bare than before.

The American taxi was parked in its usual place, but Sandrino was not there. On the north side of the piazza a souvenir shop had raised its blinds. In its window beside the cameras an assortment of goods was displayed; a flask of wine, a photograph album, ear-rings made from sea shells, clocks, embroidered bags, a statue of Neptune, lace handkerchiefs, bracelets made from fake antique coins engraved with the bearded profiles of Ulysses and Achilles.

'Yes,' said Pasquale, 'luckily tourism has arrived even here.'

But there was a note of sadness or resignation in his voice. He was thinking, no doubt, of his unsold tin icons, and the postcards yellowed by the passing seasons, hanging on the walls of his shop.

I asked him to take me to a good restaurant, if he knew of one, and to keep me company at lunch there. Pasquale Lacerba bowed with a smile. He pretended, or so it seemed to me, to hesitate and then decided to accept, though first he

39

would have to find a child to send to his home to tell his wife.

I sat down at Nicolino's, and waited for him to return. Without thinking, I ordered more ouzo. It was the first word that came to my lips, and when the glass was there on the tray in front of me it was too late to change my mind. I took a sip. At least, I hoped it would serve to chase away the thoughts of death which had filled my head since our visit to the Casetta Rossa.

CHAPTER SEVEN

1

'THE SUN,' said Pasquale Lacerba, and the island glittered before us. The sombre waters turned to silver and the two arms of land which embraced the bay were transformed from grey to pale green. On the far shore Lixourion could be seen and above it on the mountain the ruins of old villages which had been destroyed and never rebuilt, the track of a road and man-made clearings which might have been gun emplacements.

The wind had dropped and there was a good fresh smell of sea and sun mixed with the heavy scent of aloes, pine trees and drying earth.

We walked along by the sea towards the bridge which joined the two encircling arms of the bay some hundred yards from the point where the sea ended and meadows took the place of water.

Even on the asphalt of the road there were pebbles and clumps of grass washed there by the night's rain. The wooden booths that looked out on to the harbour had opened their shutters and inside people could be seen seated at tables drinking. Others, mostly old women dressed in black with scarves on their heads, were walking along the road towards the bus station, a freshly painted, arcaded building from where the little dusty buses, blue and yellow, and the big American taxis were setting out for the Aghios Gerasimos monastery.

'Hey,' cried Sandrino, leaning from the window of his taxi, 'do you want a ride up to the monastery? There are two seats going, fifty drachmae.'

Four old women and an old man with white whiskers were already squeezed on the back seat. They turned their faces towards the window fearfully, in silence, without understanding. Beside the driver on the front seat there were two boys with shaven heads and apprehensive eyes.

'Come on, there's plenty of room,' said Sandrino. I shook my head, and Pasquale Lacerba, who had seen my gesture, raised his stick. 'No,' he said, 'we are going for a walk.' 'All the way to the monastery?' asked Sandrino in amazement. 'All the way to the Italian cemetery,' replied Pasquale Lacerba. Sandrino was smiling in invitation, but his smile faded. 'It won't be as interesting as the festa at the monastery,' he said.

Pasquale Lacerba nodded, as though he agreed, but the corners of his mouth turned down and his face took on an expression between resignation and disgust. 'Do you expect us to go in this thing?' he asked. The big car shot off in a cloud of blue smoke. The photographer shrugged his shoulders. 'Calls himself a chauffeur!' he said.

We were making our way to the Italian cemetery which Pasquale Lacerba explained was across on the other side of the bay beneath the ruins of an old sea mill. Already we could make out a chapel, a little church and a house on the road which wound through the olive trees.

I had no real reason for deciding to go there, for there was nothing left to be seen. The cemetery where once the bodies, recovered from the communal ditches and the wells, had been buried must now be empty. Years before, I remembered, the remains had been exhumed and taken back to Italy on a warship.

There would be nothing to see except the gravestones, the crosses and the earth that had enclosed some nameless bones. But all the same I decided to go if only to see the soil that might have given a resting place to my father's body. Pasquale Lacerba had agreed without enthusiasm.

'We shall find Padre Armao there,' he said dejectedly. 'The Capucin friar.' Before we left the restaurant he had tried tactfully to alter our programme. 'Why don't we go and see the festa at the monastery?' he had said. 'It's a traditional peasant fête,' he had added to encourage me.

He had already suggested a visit to the festa that morning,

42

but I had forgotten about it. I was not going to waste time on a festa, particularly now that the sun had come out and, I had to admit, the island was completely transformed, clear and fresh like a jewel.

When we were half way across the bridge we stopped. Around us Cefalonia stretched out its two arms towards the dazzling sea, which made me screw up my eyes and shade them with my hand. Thousands of little beams of light were flashing, multiplying themselves, feeding on each other, vanishing. From the bridge Cefalonia seemed newly risen from the sea, dripping with water and light like some mystic god.

'You see,' said Pasquale Lacerba, stretching out his arms as though it was all his own work. 'Is it possible?' I asked. But Pasquale Lacerba, not understanding what I meant, replied, 'Of course. Didn't I tell you that in the sunshine everything about Cefalonia changed?' 'Is it possible?' I said again, in a whisper. Was it possible that amidst so much beauty such a slaughter had taken place?

CHAPTER EIGHT

1

WE REACHED the Italian cemetery on the slope of the hill. It stood in the midst of olive trees at the edge of the road to the monastery. The broken down boundary wall around it had lost its gate. Inside there were two tall dark cypress trees. Opposite, on the other side of the road, rose the higher wall of the British cemetery. Its well kept gate was fastened with a padlock. Beside the wall was the church which we had seen from the bridge. Further on, at the curve of the road, was a small pink prefabricated house.

We stopped at the entrance to the cemetery. It was easy to cross its threshold but I felt as though my legs were tied. From where we were I could see it all. The cemetery looked more like a ploughed field than a graveyard. The chapel's four ruined walls, with its painted cupola still intact like some grotesque biretta, faced the olive trees with open graves around them.

Here, in one of these holes, my father's body, nameless, without identity, that of an unknown soldier, might have been laid.

We heard a sound of steps behind us. A Capucin monk was bearing down upon us like a gust of wind, his long beard flowing before him, his eyes bright and smiling, his grey robe flapping like a sail.

'Padre Armao,' the photographer said mournfully. The friar looked at me from the height of his bony frame, his beard nodding in approval at my presence in the cemetery. It was as though he had been expecting me for a long time and at last I had arrived to end his vigil.

44

'Italian, n'est ce pas?' he asked. He was delighted at not being overlooked. He seized my hand and shook it. He inquired about where I had come from, my home town, and the sea crossing. He spoke a strange mixture of Italian, French and Spanish.

He asked me why I had come to Cefalonia; if I were a relation of one of those who had died on the island, and when I told him that my father had been among them, the light in his eyes faded, the smile that had divided his face in two disappeared and his look became sad.

'Come and have a cup of coffee,' he said to change the subject, and indicated the little red building.

Pasquale Lacerba looked straight in front of him as though to remind me that he had warned me that this Capucin monk would not easily be shaken off. He looked at me and then looked at Padre Armao without enthusiasm. 'We climbed all the way up here to see the graves,' he said.

Padre Armao moved into the cemetery and went along the main path; his robe blowing out in the wind brushed the headstones and the crosses. When he reached the middle of the cemetery, he stopped dramatically and invited us with arms flung wide to enter.

'He is my parish priest,' Pasquale Lacerba whispered hoarsely behind me. 'I'm one of his parishioners. We're just a handful in the midst of all these Greeks.' Padre Armao must have had sharp ears because he heard what had been said. He swung round on his sandals and pointing at the photographer with the forefinger of a huge hand which protruded from a vast sleeve, said, 'Few but good, with the exception of Pasquale Lacerba.' 'I am lame,' he protested. 'My health is in a bad way.'

Padre Armao gave a derisive laugh and looked at him with displeasure. 'Lame, lame!' he shouted. 'Too lame to come to church, but not too lame to go to cafés.' It was plain that the priest was not really angry with his parishioner and was enjoying rebuking him. Then he remembered that he was in the cemetery, or perhaps that I was the son of one of those who had lain there, and suddenly became thoughtful again.

45

He made a solemn gesture around with his arm. 'Vous voyez,' he said.

There was little trace of those who had lain there. Grass was climbing over the remains of the dark marble headstones whose surfaces were corroded in places and covered with green moss. There were no names carved on them, but only dates, and they were almost illegible. Some graves had no stones, but only crosses of wood or metal strips. These were black and rusty, weathered by the rain and the sun.

Padre Armao explained to me that in this cemetery the bodies of fifteen hundred Italian soldiers had been buried, and that they, together with those recovered from Zante, Ithaca and Santa Maura, as well as from the Greek front, had been transported to Italy. He asked me if my father's remains had been taken back to Italy.

I replied, officially yes, but I did not know for certain. Officially my father rested in the great white cemetery in Bari. He had been allotted a place in the long line reserved for officers. But I could not have said for certain if it really was his body or not. Nor could my mother have known. She had only seen a little wooden box hermetically sealed. And besides, even if that box had been opened before her eyes, how would she have been able to recognize its contents as being my father?

Padre Armao sighed and shook his head.

'We are still in time if we want to go to the festa,' said Pasquale Lacerba. 'There's a bus coming up the hill now.'

CHAPTER NINE

1

PADRE ARMAO'S livingroom was like Katerina's. It had prefabricated walls and the same sunblinds which moved with
every breeze on the windows, though Padre Armao's gave on
the wall of the British cemetery and the broken soil of the
Italian cemetery instead of pine trees and the bay. But for
the rest it was much the same, even to the dresser, the table
with the crocheted centre piece in the middle of the room and
the sofa, blue not red, against the wall.

He had asked us to have a taste of his liqueur. He poured
it out into two cut glasses from an almost full bottle.
The liqueur, he explained, was made from certain herbs and
roots which he had collected himself, and he himself had dis-
tilled it with his own hands. It was green, thick and very
sweet.

But this was not enough. He continued to rummage about
in the dresser in search of something else to offer us. He
took a handful of blue sugared almonds from a box and passed
them under our noses so that we had to eat some.

He explained that they were a present from a Cefaliot
couple whom he was going to marry the next Sunday. He
laughed as he spoke, moving about the tiny room, filling it
completely with his masterful presence. His long robe whisked
restlessly from corner to corner.

Who were the engaged couple, Pasquale Lacerba asked
eagerly, and where did they live?

Padre Armao told him and the photograper wrote down
the name and address on a piece of paper. It struck me that
his face which had been looking disgruntled now looked hap-

pier. 'Photos, eh?' said Padre Armao with a crafty look.

He gave Pasquale Lacerba a slap on the back which shook him as if he were a wooden doll. Then he turned to me, winking at Pasquale, and added, 'He is always after weddings. Weddings and christenings, first communions and funerals. Yes, il vient dans l'église. Alors, il est un bon catholique.'

Pasquale Lacerba had lost his air of gloom. The possibility of a photographic opportunity had brought back the glitter to his eyes behind the lenses of his spectacles, and had made him forget his disappointment about the festival at the monastery.

We had a second glass and then Padre Armao accompanied us a little way through the olive trees, as far as the road and then as far as the walls of the two cemeteries.

He remained there as we went down the road, with his hand raised, a tall dark figure with the sunlight on him and his cemeteries and his solitude.

I looked at my watch. It was too late now to catch a bus or find Sandrino's taxi. Pasquale Lacerba seemed to guess my thoughts, and said, 'The procession is over by now. But this evening there is the competition between the two brass bands.'

'What two bands?' I asked, pretending to be interested. Pasquale Lacerba laughed. 'The prettiest girls from Argostolion and Lixourion,' he said, and waited for my reaction, for any sign of interest or excitement.

'Ah!' I said.

'You will come and watch?' he went on hopefully. He awaited my reply with ill-concealed anxiety. And then: 'It is no good always thinking about death and the past. The past is past and the dead are better off than the living.'

PART TWO

CHAPTER TEN

1

ALDO PUGLISI had travelled thousands of miles from Milan to Cefalonia, by sea, through mountain passes, down valleys, along river beds, and for what? To find himself one evening seated at a well-worn wooden table in a little kitchen with whitewashed walls; an empty fireplace in front of him; and behind him a glass-fronted cupboard filled with some family photographs mixed up with the best china.

He was sitting there, wanting only to enjoy the well-earned rest of the victorious soldier, when suddenly he had detected familiar smells, bread, sifted flour, red wine spilt in the tiled passage.

At that point he had started to understand. Laying his pistol on top of the table, which was primitively made but scrubbed as white as bread, he realized that in spite of having worn many different uniforms, he was no sort of conqueror. He was just Captain Aldo Puglisi, or better still, Aldo Puglisi, the engineer, with a wife waiting for him at home and a small son whose features he could recall only with difficulty.

As far as he was concerned, from the moment that he had set foot on Cefalonia the war had been finished. 'I shall come home unscathed now; you can be sure of that,' he had written to his wife. To reassure her, because she knew on which of the islands the division had landed, he had added a few touches of local colour: Cefalonia in the late spring was all green and grey. The olive trees were silver against the sky and on the summit of a mountain there was the squat mass of an old Venetian fortress. Argostolion was a pleasant town, glittering in the sunlight. It had paved alleyways climbing up a hill and old baroque houses. In the centre was the Piazza Valianos, lined with palm trees, benches and old fashioned gas lamps. On Sundays the divisional band gave concerts in the middle of the piazza.

'The inhabitants are well disposed towards us, in their way,' Aldo Puglisi had written. 'The war is only an unhappy memory between us. I want the Greeks to forget that we ever fought against them. Even the silly old schoolmistress, Katerina Pariotis, in whose house I am billeted, understands that we are not enemies . . .'

But on this point he had not written quite truthfully. It had taken the young Greek primary schoolteacher quite a long time to understand it. On the evening of their first meeting in the dusk-filled livingroom, the captain has put some bread and some tins of food on the table, feeling almost ashamed beneath her cold and hostile stare which warned him that the usual courtesies would be useless.

Embarrassed he had said, 'Take them, Kyria. They're for you. I do not want to sleep in your house by right of conquest. I want to pay you rent. Do you understand?'

But no, Katerina Pariotis had looked at him without sympathy; not with fear, but with contempt in her dark eyes that were too big for so small a face.

'You are the master,' she said.

She waited in the shadow in the corner of the room with her face towards the window so that the foreign captain should not see it. She was thinking, 'Now he will act as if it were his own bed that he was going to sleep in.' What would not these Italians lay claim to now? They had come into other people's houses, requisitioned the best rooms, and had taken away oil and wine. They had forbidden her, a Greek schoolmistress, to teach Greek history to her pupils.

'No, Kyria, that's not true at all,' the captain had replied in a sad voice.

Even so, she could not bring herself to say anything more to him. All round her, she knew of the hunger of the Greek people and she knew of the hunger that existed in this very room. Through the doorway to the kitchen the old Pariotises could be seen looking at the bread and the tins on the table, lying on a centrepiece crocheted by Katerina. She, too, looked at the room and noticed that the flowers in the glass vase were dead. How long was it since she had last done them? She looked at the big clock on the wall across the room. It had stopped, and hung there, black, motionless against the faded pink wallpaper.

The captain said good night, and went out into the dark, disappointed because she had called him master.

It was only in regard to Katerina that Aldo Puglisi had evaded the truth. The rest of his letter was in keeping with the facts. On Cefalonia the war was just an ugly memory. It was something which they knew was still going on elsewhere, but a long way off. At the most it was something to be seen occasionally on the horizon in the smoke of an enemy flotilla steaming towards some distant objective. Even less often the sea was suddenly lit up at night. On those occasions the war away on the skyline did seem more of a reality. White flashes from the guns flickered like gas lamps in a storm, for an instant blotting out the stars in the sky and revealing an expanse of livid sea. But even then, it was a war without sound, almost nonexistent. The soldiers and the Cefaliots watched these naval engagements from the hill tops or from Capo San Teodoro amidst the flowering aloes and broom and from the houses and villages lying on the eastern slope of the island until they faded out or disappeared into the distance.

Would any of them have been sunk, the Italians and Captain Aldo Puglisi wondered?

Katerina Pariotis, who used to watch the flashes through the slats of the shutters, hoped so, and that a lot of Italian ships would have been sent to the bottom by the British, and to this end she prayed fervently to the icons of her saints.

A more frequent occurrence was the sounding of the air raid alarm by the ships in the harbour. But even this was of no real importance. It was as though they were playing some game. The Anglo-American formations would pass high above Cefalonia. People used to count them; twenty-nine, thirty, forty, sometimes even a hundred or more. Heavily loaded,

53

they moved slowly as though they found it tiring to get above the island's mountains, and might at any moment fall, even though the anti-aircraft guns were not firing. They came from beyond the sea in waves, like migrating birds. The noise of the engines made the window panes rattle and the plates and glasses on the dresser and in the sideboard vibrate.

But it was not war. After a time, the soldiers and the islanders got used to the planes and gave up following the path of their flight and counting them with the curiosity that they had shown at the start. The formations came and went as though they did not even see the island with its batteries and its tiny fleet of boats anchored in the waters of the bay.

'They are our liberators,' Katerina Pariotis used to say to her pupils as she stood near the window pointing into the air. 'Don't forget it. One day those people up there will come to free us.'

But even to her it seemed impossible that one day the island would have to be liberated by a real battle, real war between the British and the Italians. Cefalonia was too mild and pleasant a place to support the weight of a war. The Italians had descended from the sky and landed from the sea without a shot fired, and looking at the receding bombers Katerina hoped that they would return home in the same way.

'Miss, is it true that we must hate the Italians?'

'Yes, it is, but who told you that?'

'Must we hate them when they give us bread?'

'We must hate them all the time.'

Even though they gave them bread and tins of meat and sang their love songs at night in the dark alleyways of Argostolion; even though sometimes coming out of school the children saw them hoeing in the fields and the vineyards as though they were the elder brothers or fathers who had gone away to fight, they must be hated because of the war which had been of their making; because a certain Aldo Puglisi was sleeping in the narrow iron bed with the medallion of the Madonna painted at the head which had been bought for Katerina Pariotis as a child. For these reasons and many others which the children could not yet understand, they had to be hated.

54

'We must hate them without telling anyone,' Katerina Pariotis would say.

At midday the school closed, and the children ran off shouting, dashing down the cobbled alleys. In order to avoid climbing the paths through the hills which were long and tiring, Katerina had to cross Piazza Valianos to reach her home on the other side of the town on the road to Capo San Teodoro. She used to hurry across the piazza, her head held high, her unsmiling gaze fixed straight ahead so as not to see the Italian officers with the local girls and other people who kept company with them. At that time of day they were all there. There were the two Karamelli sisters wandering in and out of the shops or just looking in their windows. Pasquale Lacerba the photographer was seated amidst his fellow countrymen waving his arms about like a puppet. There were the four or five divisional prostitutes, Italians too, seated at café tables with their legs crossed, the better to show them off, as though that was still necessary. They were smoking, laughing and drinking ouzo and water from big glasses. They looked like dolls made of straw, so painted were they, red and black with their hair brightly peroxided.

Captain Aldo Puglisi was there. He rose from his seat when he saw her and gave a half bow. But Katerina Pariotis almost started to run to escape from the stares. She felt them boring into her back. She felt soiled and mocked.

'The pretty little schoolteacher,' one of them said.

For a moment they watched her in silence, eagerly following the supple movement of her slender body, more like that of a girl than a woman, as she disappeared down the eucalyptus avenue.

'No poaching,' someone said.

'No, no,' protested Aldo Puglisi. 'She is a good girl, I assure you.'

The officers started to laugh. The girls joined in more from spite than because they were offended. 'Hear that, what about us?' they cried, looking round them with their great mascaraed eyes. 'Aren't we good girls?'

Yes, they were good girls. They were doing their duty.

Every morning they were up early and climbed into trucks. All day they raced here and there about the island, up hill and down dale, visiting the different units. When night fell, they returned to their villa and with aching bones threw themselves exhausted on their beds. And when at last they thought they were going to rest and drowsiness had overtaken them, the voice of Signora Nina would call up the stairs and drag them back to reality.

'Girls, will you come down please?'

In the living-room on the ground floor, in the orange light of the shaded lamp, there was a throng of yet more soldiers.

'Don't we fight for our country?' asked Adriana.

In the peaceful, simple world of Cefalonia, it was only for them that the war was still going on, just as it had been in Africa and everywhere else they had been sent.

CHAPTER ELEVEN

1

FOR ANYONE who had come from six months in the African desert, as had Adriana and her colleagues, Argostolion seemed a real metropolis. It was a city full of crowded, noisy streets. There were cafés with tables out on the pavements, shop windows glittering in the sunshine, and street crossings where the traffic stopped at a sign from the military police. When, after six months of flat, grey, unfriendly desert, huts in the back areas, and the rumble of gunfire, Adriana and her companions had stepped ashore on to the quayside of the harbour, they had looked around them with weary eyes and had noted with approval the ridge of hills dark with olive groves and pinewoods lying beyond the green roofs and bell towers of the town.

'What's it look like to you, girls?' Adriana had said with her straw bag slung over her shoulder, her long thin legs wide apart like a soldier standing at ease. 'Doesn't it look just as if it had been made to measure for us?'

An abandoned villa with a garden in front of it on the other side of the bay, opposite the town but some way from it, had been got ready for them. The walls were pale blue and the shutters were a faded green. The house was hardly visible behind clumps of aloes and a high stone wall, and from the road to Lixourion only the upper floor and the roof could be seen.

For some days they had allowed themselves a complete rest to recover their strength.

Each morning, in a creaking horse carriage driven by Matias, a retired sailor, they had driven down to the town across the long bridge which lay over the water. The carriage, its lively passengers and the flower-like flutterings of their parasols were reflected in the sea, whilst high up on the box Matias nodded his head in time with his horse.

In the afternoons with the shutters closed against the blaze of the summer sun, they shut themselves in their rooms. Stretched out on their narrow hospital beds, they read and sipped tall glasses of iced coffee, or they came downstairs to play cards in the livingroom beside the lifeless radio set.

Through the slats of the shutters their eyes were dazzled by the luminous, still sea. They could see the shore of the bay, the harbour, and the warships at anchor. Often a squad of soldiers would appear on the stretch of sandy beach not far distant from the villa. They used to come running like boys from school. Chattering, they would undress hurriedly, the sun accentuating their nakedness. Then, dressed only in their white underpants, waving their arms in the air, they would plunge into the sea, raising a mist of golden spray around them.

But none of the girls wanted to stand there and watch them. They were fed up to the teeth with men; soldiers in particular. If, for a moment, one of them did glance through the shutters, it was because she did not know what to do between one game of cards and the next, between reading a newspaper days old and drinking another glass of bad coffee. To look at soldiers bathing was no more entertaining than lying on one's back and gazing at the ceiling.

At times Adriana spent hours gazing at her ceiling. Round its four corners garlands of wild flowers climbed. She looked at the ceiling and all the while made a little current of air with a mother of pearl fan, decorated with painted figures. It was a present from Signora Nina. She had given one to each of the girls so that in the quiet of the afternoon when voices and footsteps were still the weary fluttering of the fans could be heard through the silence.

How unpredictable was the course of life, Adriana thought. She saw it all again, as though it were a film projected on the ceiling; so many pictures recalled all at once, superimposed one on the other, but each one sharp and distinct: Giuseppa's tailor's shop, the Sunday visits to the cinema, the walks with her girl friends down to the level crossing, the three-piece bands in the smoky workers' clubs. 'Who could have told me,' she said, 'that the path from that first hotel bedroom would have ended on Cefalonia?' Depression changed to sadness and an unexplained desire to weep.

To break her chain of thoughts, she jumped off her bed, glanced into the looking glass and touched up her lips. She lit a cigarette to calm herself. Nothing was going to happen to her here, protected by these homely reassuring walls. The warships were in the harbour and there were the supply depots, the vehicle parks, the encampments and the gun positions. It was just a jolly camping holiday, albeit, like many things which men did, deprived of any sense. The soldiers were just peasants in uniform who idled away their time working on the island's smallholdings and the officers were just boisterous students on holiday, come to play a harmless game on an island all their own.

She dressed, looking all the while in the mirror for signs of growing old, of another day passed.

From the room next door the girl from Trieste knocked on the wall to ask if she was ready to go to the beach.

Protected from the sun by their flower-covered sunshades, they teetered on high heels down the road to the now deserted beach. Their long shadows cast before them moved awkwardly like caricatures. 'See what we look like,' said la Triestina.

Their legs were bare to the knee and their skirts were very tight. Their appearance contrasted strangely with their parasols which belonged to another age and another world having nothing in common with bare legs and clinging skirts.

'We are real whores,' said LaTriestina with a strangely satisfied air. 'It is no good wanting to go for a walk like a lady, we are just whores.'

Peasants in the fields and vineyards turned to gaze at them and followed them with astonished looks. 'They're always working, these Turks,' La Triestina said. One of them climbed a wall to see them better.

A lorry passed and the two women stood to one side at the verge of the road. As soon as the soldiers in the back of the vehicle recognized them, there was a chorus of catcalls and they leant out and waved. 'Going to bathe, my beauties?' they cried. 'Can we lend you a hand?'

Adriana smiled. What if they jeered at her now, when in a few days' time they would be around as meek as lambs queueing up for her favours? But LaTriestina went pale with anger, and her bronzed face turned livid. She put her hands to her mouth and with the sinews of her neck standing out shouted, 'Go and lend your sisters a hand!'

In her agitation she had dropped her parasol, and the wind from the lorry blew it down the road. Amidst the laughter of the disappearing soldiers they both started to run after it. La Triestina stopping in the middle of the road, tall as a guardsman, her well developed bosom heaving from exertion. She shook her fist at the sky, but had no more breath to shout.

'Damned cretins,' she hissed between her teeth, 'and to think that it's for their benefit that we are here in this cesspit of an island.'

Cefalonia seemed to fade in the afternoon heat. The water of the bay took on the white colour of the sky and the distant mountains and hills smoking in a blue haze seemed to float in mid air.

2

The officers and the girls had called him Nicolino, because he was small and comic, with timid eyes; but he was cunning, too. Hardly would they have sat down at the tables of his café when he would appear, always ready on his toes, always attentive, always with an air of familiar complicity.

'Madame?' he would say to the girls, and to the officers 'Messie?' as he waited for their orders.

Adriana thought he was pulling their legs when he called them 'madame'. The only one who really believed him was Signora Nina. She liked Nicolino because, sincere or not, he had a way with him and knew how to treat women.

'He is a very well mannered Greek,' she used to say.

When the girls laughed after a glass or two of ouzo, or the officers laughed, Nicolino started to laugh as well, to please them, because they had defeated his nation and he was frightened of them.

'You're a fine fellow,' LaTriestina used to say, slapping him on the back.

'Yes, Madame,' he would reply, and then unexpectedly 'Viva il Duce, viva!' he would say, and come to attention, his face suddenly serious, looking over the rooftops around the piazza.

'Go on with you,' LaTriestina used to reply, 'if you could get away with it you would kill us all, and all the officers too, wouldn't you?'

Nicolino, terrified, used to bend over the tables wiping a dirty rag across the wooden surfaces, picking up and setting down the glasses. 'Madame,' he would say under his breath, 'I am Fascist. All Italian officers know. Me their friend.'

'Bravo, you little pimp!' LaTriestina hissed between her teeth.

3

He heard the sound of the little aluminium hydroplane which took off every morning for a reconnaissance flight round the bay. From the harbour a destroyer's hooter sounded. From somewhere, the barracks or the hillside, came a babble of voices, singing broke out, and from here and there came the report of a shot. He ran across the livingroom to the window which gave on to the road and found himself elbow to elbow at the window sill with Katerina Pariotis.

'Kalimera, Kyria,' he said.

Katerina leant out of the window and looked towards the city, but she could see nothing and turned away in silence.

The captain sat down at the table on which, amongst the litter of Katerina's books and a vase of fresh flowers, was a wireless set. He switched it on and nervously tried to tune in to one of the Italian stations or any other station, even one that was hostile, but all he could get was atmospherics or ships' signals in morse code.

Katerina had realized that something was going on amongst the Italians. Since the day when the Anglo-Americans had landed in Sicily there had been no singing in the streets at night, and on Sundays in Piazza Valianos there had been less animation and the concerts given by the military band had been less gay, or so it had seemed to her. The captain had been looking sad. She often felt his eyes upon her through the open door but she had to admit that they were kind eyes in search of friendship or even just a kind word. Every night before he shut himself in his room, he left bread and tins on the table, and each morning he left the house with a simple 'good morning'. If the old lady thanked him, he would smile and look guilty. 'What for?' he would say, as though he was ashamed. Then he used to jump on to his motorcycle and ride off amidst a cloud of smoke and the smell of petrol.

Suddenly the captain's hands were still. Amongst the countless signals they had found an Italian station. He got up, while a voice continued to speak. Katerina watched him as she leant against the door frame and behind her the old people watched him from the kitchen. They, too, realized that something was happening or had already happened.

'Mussolini has been arrested,' the captain said to no one in particular. The Italian voice stopped and the sittingroom was filled by the sound of martial music. To Katerina it seemed as though the waves of sound lifted her from the floor and carried her up high. She wanted to cry out, to run and do something, but a feeling of embarrassment restrained her and kept her in the kitchen doorway looking at the captain. He went to finish shaving and she heard the familiar sounds from his room. This was the day for which she had been waiting ever since the occupation had started. She ought to have wanted to shout at him 'And now are you going home again? Can I sleep in my own bed again?' or 'Captain, can I teach Greek history and their language to my pupils once again?'

But the words would not come to her lips. They formed themselves in her brain, but she lacked the will to utter them. The captain came back into the living-room. He was dressed in his smart uniform, but he looked tired and his eyes were sadder than ever.

He stopped in front of Katerina, trying to find something to say to her. 'For us Italians, the war will soon be over,' he said, and then forcing a smile, 'Are you glad?' he asked.

For a moment his eyes met hers and then he went out quickly, saying, as he said every morning, 'Kalimera, Kyria.'

4

All she needed to have said to cheer him up was 'Kalimera, Kapitanos'. Why hadn't she answered him?

The beach was not quite empty. Two of the Italian girls were undressing behind a clump of aloes. Katerina sat down on a stone and took off her sandals.

Had she really come down to the beach just to say good morning to him?

Katerina looked at the sea sloping away above the top of lighthouse to the horizon. The two girls were standing on a rock. They had taken off all their clothes. They were naked and the shape of their bronzed bodies was sharply outlined against the sky. The taller of the two had the robust physique of a classical statue. They were joking and laughing. Then they ran leaping from rock to rock, and threw themselves into the sea. They disappeared and reappeared further out in the sparkling waters of the bay shimmering like fish. Side by side they swam, describing a great circle in the sea plunging and leaping as they went. From time to time they paused to float on their backs and to draw breath, blowing water high into the air whilst seagulls wheeled around them.

Katerina opened her book and read a few words, but the light reflected by the sea was too strong. The heat was stifling and somnolence crept over her, encouraging idleness.

When the captain came on to the beach she would say, 'Kalimera, Kapitanos', because she was not capable of bearing ill will toward a stranger in misfortune, even though he be an enemy. Aldo Puglisi would arrive at any moment, she knew. She had often seen him with his orderly sitting on this stretch of beach.

She shut her eyes and placed a handkerchief over them to keep out the sun. Through her closed eyelids and the printed material the sky seemed dark yellow, almost orange. She sensed someone behind her. She turned round to look, and there was Captain Puglisi.

Dark glasses hid a good part of his face but she had recognized him by the sad way he had of smiling. Standing on the rocks he seemed taller than he really was. He was wearing khaki shorts and a white army shirt with the collar unbuttoned. His thin legs were dark with hair as was his chest which showed in the opening of his shirt. A little way behind him stood his orderly, Gerace, a little man even darker than the captain, a sort of shadow drawn from the rocks.

'Kalimera, Kapitanos,' said Katerina. Had she really said it, she asked herself, or only thought she had? Perhaps she had only thought it, because the captain remained silent behind her, as though he was uncertain if he should come closer.

He saw the two girls come out of the sea and go towards the aloes where their clothes showed white in the sun. One of them knotted a towel round her waist, while the other flung her arms open and did exercises bending and stretching, completely naked. He saw her throw back the hair that had fallen over her face, and blow her nose between two fingers. Then she turned her back to them and sat down beside her friend. She stretched herself out flat with her face to the sun and gently stroked the nipples of her breast.

'Gesu!' Gerace exclaimed.

Katerina heard the captain move and he sat down some

feet away from her. Scarcely turning her head, so that he would not notice, she tried to look where he was but she could only see his shadow lying close to her. She wondered why he had not sat beside her. Could he really not have heard her 'Kalimera, Kapitanos'?

He turned towards her. His mouth broke into a smile, but it was as if he was smiling at something and not at someone. He had a book in his hand but he had not opened it. He looked at Katerina's slender neck, with her hair drawn back at the nape, her small bony shoulders, full of obstinacy, and her little secret body bursting with hostility. He did not know that the hostility was gone now that he was in trouble.

The orderly remained standing on a rock some way off, leering through screwed eyes at the girl's naked body glittering in the sun with every movement. She turned on her side and then lay face downwards, with her head on her folded arms. She looked lazily at Katerina, the captain, and Gerace, with his soft black moustache, drooping over the corners of his mouth, which he stroked incessantly with nervous fingers. Suddenly the girl jumped to her feet and moved over the rocks towards the aloes, her breasts swinging at every step. She lit a cigarette and standing up blew smoke rings in the air. Without moving his eyes from the girl Gerace lit one, too. The whiteness of her teeth, the flash of her eyes and the smoky black of her hair made her seem like a great cat. She sat down hugging her legs to her breasts, her chin on her knees.

Why had she come to the beach if she was not going to speak to him? Katerina wondered. She could not have said 'Kalimera' after all, she was quite sure, otherwise he would not now be sitting there silent and distant. She had come to the beach to look for him and she had behaved like a silly child.

She sighed. The hot air smelt of rocks and salt. Capo San Teodoro seemed to float out at sea, quivering in the light.

The captain, too, had tried to read but he had shut his book and left it lying on his knees. He was looking at the angular figure, full of unfriendliness. Why had he had two copies made of the photograph? He glanced at them concealed between two pages of his book. 'One for your wife and one for your girlfriend', the photographer had said to him, and he thought how absurd it all was, to presume to thank someone whom you had conquered and humiliated, and expect her to speak to you when you were sleeping in her bed without her permission, to expect friendship from a people upon whom you had made war, even though once in their homes, you did give them something to lessen their hunger.

'With friendship and asking forgiveness to Katerina Pariotis from an Italian officer.' He reread the inscription written across the photograph. Yes, it was both absurd and ridiculous. But Katerina might at least know before their departure that he had wanted nothing more from her than a friendly word. How could he explain to her all his feelings of guilt and shame and of affection too? He could not go back to Italy leaving silence and ill feeling behind him, for lack of having told her of the sympathy that he felt for her, her parents, the people of the island, and for all the Greek people and the Greek heritage.

He reached out towards her and touched her lightly on the shoulder with the photograph. Katerina took it without surprise, as though she had been waiting for it. She looked at it for a long moment, bent over it, deciphering the words and taking in their meaning. 'She is going to tear it up,' he thought. But Katerina smiled at him. 'Thank you,' she said, and put the photograph between the pages of her book.

'That's better,' the captain thought, and so did Katerina. They both turned away and looked in front of them as though a weight had been taken from them.

In the shadow of the aloe the two girls were dressing with what seemed to be calculated slowness. Gerace continued to stare at them, squatting on a stone, while his cigarette end burnt down between his fingers.

5

Units of German infantry and artillery had landed on the first of August. In the morning the girls at the villa heard them approaching from the direction of Lixourion down the road to Argostolion. There was a sound of engines, different to the noise of the Italian vehicles to which they were accustomed. They ran to the window and watched the bend in the road where the summer heat danced in a shimmering haze on the hard surface. They waited, watching curiously. The noise came closer and grew louder. Then they saw why it was they had not recognized the sound.

The first to appear round the corner were two motor-cyclists balancing themselves against the camber of the road. They split the dancing heat, straightened out, and passed at speed in a flash. A truck with a low, snoutlike radiator which appeared to be eating the dust followed them. Then came other motorcycles clinging to the curve of the road. They shot by in a blast of wind. The glint of metal and the reflection of the light from their shuttered headlamps seemed to increase their number, and an acrid smell of petrol fumes filled the air.

'Germans,' Signora Nina said quietly and was silent. She stared towards the town chewing nervously at the black bone handle of her parasol. She did not like Germans. She could not stand their gross, coarse ways. 'They're no gentlemen,' she had always said.

The flashes of light and their attendant shadows moved swiftly along the road. The women and the peasants out in the fields saw and heard them. Katerina Pariotis saw them, too, from her window, and her heart beat fast with alarm.

The Germans passed quickly by the villa. In a car camouflaged in yellow, maroon and green so that it looked like some monstrous toad, sat four fair-haired officers. Adriana saw their expression, the cold hard German stare, but she got only a fleeting impression as they did not turn their heads. They sat with their gaze fixed towards Argostolion. They went over the bridge and disappeared from view behind the first houses of the town.

It all happened in a moment like an apparition. That was what it had seemed like to Katerina Pariotis, too, but a very solid apparition the sight of which had drained her of strength and left her empty and weak as she stood at her window.

A small E-boat slipped out of the harbour, clean and white with two whiskers of spray flying back from its bows. It slid across the sea splitting the water like a knife blade, leaving behind it a faint wake pointing towards the horizon. It turned away to the right and then to the left as though it was uncertain as to what route to select in so much space. It started to dart to and fro as if it had gone mad or was playing some game. Finally it turned and, pointing its whiskers towards the harbour, came back quietly and obediently to disappear behind the grey arm of the mole.

'Girls,' said Signora Nina, putting on her hat with the veil, 'shall we go down to the town and see what's going on?' Tall and thin, like a hatstand dressed up, puffing smoke through her nostrils, she walked down the stairs and across the garden without waiting for an answer. The girls hurried behind her like chicks after a hen, looking round anxiously for Matias and his carriage.

The town was quiet although there was quite a crowd round the piazza and there was more traffic about than usual. The German car was parked in front of the Palazzo which housed the Italian headquarters. The motorcycles were standing beneath the trees, with their riders still in the saddle.

Signora Nina and the girls were seated in front of Nicolino's café. Standing on tiptoe Nicolino looked breathlessly over their heads and could barely be persuaded to pay attention to them. 'Madame?' he said, hardly taking his eyes off the piazza for one instant while he took their order. He went into the café and was quickly back amongst the tables, with his zinc tray balanced on his finger tips, gazing all the time at the Germans.

The Germans did not move. Sitting on their motorcycles they showed no curiosity. It was as if they were alone in the piazza. They did not even look at the girls. They waited for their officers who had gone into the Italian headquarters. They waited with the patience of those accustomed to obeying orders and accustomed to doing nothing else.

'Madame,' said Nicolino as he served the glasses of ouzo.

His small hairy fist shook as he poured a little of the liquid into each glass. 'At Lixourion,' he murmured, 'they disembarked at Lixourion.' Signora Nina sat quite still. She too was staring at the corner of the square, sucking at the handle of her parasol. She gazed at the Germans like a basilisk, studying their movements. 'How many of them are there?' she asked. Nicolino bent forward and passed a cloth across the table. 'Thousands,' he said, 'they've occupied the whole island.' Signora Nina gave Nicolino a fierce look as though it was all his fault. 'And what will the Italians do?' she asked. Nicolino shrugged his shoulders, smiled and then looked serious, mopping his brow with his cloth wet with ouzo. 'They'll negotiate,' he said.

It was at this moment that Oberleutnant Karl Ritter came out into the piazza. The crowd saw the German soldiers jump off their motorcycles and stand to attention. They saw him, though they did not know his rank or who he was, move out of the shade into the sun. Slowly he walked across the piazza, a little selfconsciously, aware that all eyes were upon him. Overcoming a moment's hesitation he moved towards the tables outside Nicolino's café and for the first time noticed the presence of the girls. He turned to look at them and, seeing them for what they were, was unable to conceal a look of haughty contempt.

The words 'Gott mit uns' were plainly visible engraved on his Wehrmacht officer's belt, as was the big black leather holster with the long thin barrel of a machine pistol protruding from it hanging at his side.

He sat down facing the square at an empty table in profile to the girls. They were able to admire to the full his unusual good looks which struck them dumb and reminded them of something at the back of their minds once seen and then forgotten. His features somehow seemed familiar, like a dream that had come true.

The German soldiers returned to sitting on their motorcycles or walked around them smoking and talking in low voices. Short automatic rifles were slung across their chests. At first they had seemed harmless boys on a camping expe-

69

dition, but their charm had vanished when they had snapped to attention at the appearance of the oberleutnant.

All eyes were turned on Karl Ritter. Nicolino hurried to his side, beaming with a deferential smile. He drew himself up to attention like a musical comedy soldier and said, 'Messie!'

The oberleutnant ordered ouzo, and his glass spilled over when Nicolino put the tray down on the table. But the officer took no notice and went on looking uninterestedly around him.

Pasquale Lacerba came into the square. He bowed to Signora Nina before making his way to her side. She smiled at him distractedly, hardly taking her eyes off the piazza. He took her lace gloved hand and raised it to his lips. It was the first time that he had ever been seen to do so. He seemed more well-bred, more distinguished, and at the same time paler than ever.

'Seen this?' asked Nina, pleasantly stirred by his new gallantry. The photographer's eyes and mouth softened momentarily. His face registered a strange mixture of amusement and anxiety. 'This is just what I thought would happen,' he said, 'they don't trust the Italians any more.'

Oberleutnant Karl Ritter turned to look at them. One after the other the girls felt his blue eyes slowly passing over them and became aware of a strange inner conflict. He looked at them without any particular expression of either desire or disgust. He looked at Nina and Pasquale Lacerba and all their eyes, dark and smouldering, blue and cold, met above the tables.

'Why,' asked Nina, 'because of Badoglio?' 'That's right,' answered Pasquale, adjusting his spectacles. He seemed quite calm. The arrival of the Germans had been no surprise to him. 'The Italians are about to sign an armistice with the Allies, that's obvious,' he said.

Karl Ritter shifted uneasily on the hard wooden café chair. He felt the eyes, which had not left him since he came into the piazza, boring into him. He seemed almost smothered by their curiosity. He crossed his legs and gazed ahead of him trying to preserve his dignity. He took a white packet from his pocket and put it carelessly on the table. With a flick of his fingers he opened it and shook out an unbroken line of cigarettes. For a moment he appeared absorbed in looking at them and then with a sudden movement he turned towards the girls and offered them the packet.

'Smoke?'

'Go on, take one,' urged Pasquale seeing the girls' hesitation. Their white hands fell swiftly on the packet and a ballet of red varnished nails fluttered round the big sunburnt hand of the oberleutnant.

'Danke schön,' said Adriana, and she was the first to smile at the German. The oberleutnant noticing that only Nina did not take a cigarette thrust the packet under her nose and waited.

'Don't make a scene,' urged Pasquale, smiling as though he was saying something else. He took one, too, and said, 'Danke schön' as though he was saying it for her.

The oberleutnant's blue eyes wandered between the Italian headquarters and the girls. They rested for a moment on the long thin legs of Adriana and on the ample bosom, partly bared, of La Triestina, who breathed deeply to make it yet more prominent. She liked the cold blue stare and so did Adriana and all the girls except Signora Nina.

Katerina Pariotis had also hurried to the piazza. She wanted to see the Germans too. She looked from the headquarters to Nicolino's and realized that something irreparable was taking place notwithstanding the smiles of the Italian girls, the sun, and the quiet that hung over the town. The war was not to be over so soon after all, at least not for the Cefaliots. Even if the Italians went away, and that was certainly what they were negotiating about inside, the Germans would remain.

'These cigarettes make me retch,' said Nina, gazing at the oberleutnant through half-closed eyes. She smiled at him through clenched teeth. He smiled back and moved his attention from Adriana's legs to La Triestina's breasts.

The Karamelli sisters came into the square. They walked like a pair of well-matched horses, their bodies showing dark

71

beneath their flimsy dresses. They looked from the motorcyclists to the oberleutnant and they too were struck by his looks.

'But what is going on in there?' asked Nina. 'Why don't our people come out?'

'They are negotiating,' said Pasquale.

Signora Nina threw her half-smoked cigarette into the gutter from where it sent up a thin blue thread of smoke hardly visible in the full light of the sun which fell almost vertically on to the tarmac.

'But do you think they'll agree on something?' she asked.

'Ja,' said the lieutenant. The girls looked at him. Karl Ritter smiled, staring at Signora Nina.

'Of course they will,' said Pasquale.

Signora Nina could not hide her own surprise. She looked dejected and tired. 'You think so?' she said.

'We – allies,' said Karl Ritter, indicating the Italian headquarters with a nod of his head.

He seemed to want to make this situation clear although no one showed any signs of doubting it. 'Italians and Germans . . . friends,' he repeated.

Again the photographer spoke. 'Of course they are. Of course they are.'

'What about Badoglio?' asked Signora Nina, and her voice betrayed a tremor of hope.

The oberleutnant made a vertical pulling movement with his hand in the air.

'Scheisse,' he said.

'What's that mean?' Signora Nina asked Pasquale Lacerba.

The photographer cleared his throat and hesitated. 'He means shit, Signora Nina.'

CHAPTER TWELVE

1

WHEN THEY MET for the first time in the marquee which housed the officers' mess at Lixourion they all behaved very correctly. The rectangular tent was brightly illuminated by electric lamps. With glasses raised high above the tables, catching the light, they had drunk to the glory of their respective countries and to the success of their armies. During the meal all had been smiles and politeness. As a supper party it was a great success.

Many of the German officers spoke Italian. They came from the Tyrol and were Austrian rather than German, with red faces, fat cheeks, and slit eyes. If it had not been for the grey Wehrmacht uniform which they wore, they could have been mistaken for mountain peasants arrived on Cefalonia by mistake. They were easy people to talk to, more because of their homely features than because of the wine that they had drunk.

Leutnant Franz Fauth was seated at the centre of the table to the right of Captain Puglisi. He listened to the conversation and watched the scene absent-mindedly, drumming on the table with the fingers of his left hand, playing with the knives, lighting a cigarette and then throwing it away and grinding it into the earth floor of the tent with his heel. Captain Puglisi had the feeling that his mind was elsewhere. From time to time he pulled himself together and acknowledged the presence of the others apologetically. Then he would ask Oberleutnant Ritter who was sitting opposite him what they were talking about. With his head on one side he listened to the metallic voice of the fair-haired officer, whilst the other voices round him died down into silence. Then with a vague smile Franz Fauth would agree 'Jawohl, jawohl' to what had been said.

But amongst the German officers it was Karl Ritter who held the captain's attention. Not only because of his unusual bearing which brought to mind the warriors of classical times, but because the strange clarity of the lines of his face seemed to indicate a kind of inner dedication, elemental and savage, that bordered upon innocence. Karl Ritter talked with equal confidence on cultural subjects and the war. He propounded a series of theories which the captain found it difficult to refute, so incredible were they and stated with such candour.

Aldo Puglisi looked at him with astonishment and fascination, while for a good half hour Ritter explained how and why some races such as the Greeks must be considered as entirely negative factors in the story of civilization and human progress. He did not succeed in finding any valid arguments with which to contradict the German, but he thought of the gentleness of Katerina Pariotis, of the kindness of some of the inhabitants of Argostolion and of the whitewashed kitchens of the houses he had happened to enter.

'Those who for centuries have sunk to the level of waiters,' Ritter had concluded, 'must be kept at that level so that they do not form an obstacle to the onward march of more powerful peoples, of the master races.' 'Perhaps he is just trying to shock me,' thought Aldo Puglisi.

But the lieutenant's cold stare shattered all illusions. It was no exhibition to impress on his part. He believed in all good faith in what he had been expounding. He believed in it in all innocence and with complete sincerity.

Then Captain Puglisi looked at him and saw him as he really was. He was not a monster. His theories provoked neither disgust nor rebellion. He was simply just a poor deluded boy. All that perfection of features, colouring, and physique was only a miserable shell which hid a festering disease of which Karl Ritter himself was completely unaware.

'Sad?' Karl Ritter asked, catching his eye. The captain pointed to his uniform and then to Karl's and said, 'Perhaps it is this that makes us so powerful'. Karl Ritter smiled like a satisfied baby. He felt fine in his uniform. How many different ones had the Italians and Germans worn since they were born? Aldo Puglisi counted them to see who had worn the most and then even Karl saw the joke.

Wolf-cub, Ballila, Avanguardista, young Fascist, Guffista, young soldier, officer cadet. He catalogued all the Italian uniforms.

'They make life simpler, don't they?' he said. Karl Ritter listened to him without understanding what he was trying to say, but he nodded his head in encouragement. 'When we put on a uniform,' Aldo Puglisi went on, 'we become part of an organized body. We have finished with individuality, and at the same time we have finished with responsibility. From the moment we put on a uniform, someone does the thinking for us, someone makes plans for us, gives the orders, and makes the decisions for us. It is the end of our childhood.'

He was surprised at himself for saying this, because at the same time he was really thinking, 'From babyhood we have been doing what we are told to do, without exercising our brains one bit.'

'Is that how it seems to you?' asked Karl Ritter, the smile dying on his lips. His hard crystal gaze fixed on Aldo Puglisi as without waiting for an answer he embarked on the exposition of another of his theories. 'Uniforms,' he said, 'can be more or less ridiculous according to who wears them. But in a modern society they are indispensable if you want to unite into one the wellbeing of all its components.'

The captain said nothing and the smile returned to the German's lips. 'Therefore,' he went on, 'wearing a uniform does not make existence easier, because we wear it all the time for high motives, and because besides myself and besides you, my Italian comrade, there are cretins and village idiots wearing the same uniform. We put on uniforms to ensure their happiness.'

The conception of life which Aldo Puglisi had that evening, in the officers' mess beneath the stars on the hill at Lixourion, with the sea stretching away at his feet, was not as clear and clean cut as that of Oberleutnant Ritter. He sighed, increasingly aware of the malady that was tainting the superb animal seated opposite him. He replied simply, in a conciliatory tone of voice, that life to him at any rate did not seem quite like that.

It was different, and there he stopped, without specifying what was different.

At the end of the evening glasses were raised in a last toast and then the voices and footsteps of their German comrades were lost in the night along the paths that led to their positions. That night Aldo felt himself alone, more alone than ever after listening to the theories of Karl Ritter without confounding them. He felt uneasy as though he had betrayed Katerina's friendship.

He mounted his motorcycle and rode down to Argostolion.

2

Katerina went to the window. The captain was there, a dark outline against the brightness of the stars. She could not see his face, but she knew who it was at once. He stood in the middle of the garden path with his head raised towards the window to which she had come at the sound of the motorcycle.

'Kalispera, Kyria,' he said. 'Kalispera, Signore,' she replied. The big army motorcycle stood on the verge of the road raised on its stand with its back wheel still turning.

'I have come to look you up,' said the captain. Katerina smiled in the darkness. She was not surprised. She had expected and hoped that he would come. 'You are a persistent lodger,' she replied. It was ridiculous to be talking like this out of the window to an Italian. He looked ridiculous, too, standing down there as though he were a peasant boy beneath the window of his girl. Their words came slowly, at long intervals, because each of them was searching carefully for the right thing to say.

'No rooms to let in Lixourion?' asked Katerina. The captain came up the path. His cigarette glowed red amongst the flowers. 'It is not only that,' he answered. In the hot August night they heard the crickets singing all round them. 'What else is it?' asked Katerina. The captain stopped a few paces from the doorstep. He could not explain. He did not know himself what else it was. It was a sort of sense of guilt; the need to have a few words with her, to confirm the friendship between them and that nothing was changed now that his battery had moved to Lixourion. He felt that the Pariotis house was in some way his home.

'Would you like to go for a ride?' he asked. Katerina looked out at the empty sea behind him beyond the white road. 'I'm coming down,' she said. She found herself in the garden, surprised how easy it was, but as she followed the captain down the gravel path she felt quite weak and lightheaded.

'Where shall we go?' he asked. But it did not matter where they went. The important thing was that she was out at that hour with Captain Aldo Puglisi, who had once been her enemy.

Seated on the wide pillion, as comfortable as an armchair, she felt the power of the engine between her knees. Her whole body vibrated while the blue exhaust smoke which escaped beneath her feet vanished behind them.

The night parted before them as they rode. The wind beat on their faces and ruffled their hair. The speed and the wind made her want to sing, a thing which she had had no urge to do since before the war. She beat on the captain's back with her fists. 'Faster,' she shouted, but the wind whipped the words from her mouth and he did not hear them.

They stopped by the sea mills. The stars above the squat buildings and the calm sea had become bright and solid. The captain got down and pulled the motorcycle up on to its stand with Katerina still on the pillion seat. He stood beside her, his face level with hers. 'Well?' he asked. Katerina felt afraid. 'Well what?' she replied. Aldo Puglisi scratched his head, not knowing where to look. 'Well, nothing.' he said. He looked at Katerina's head, small and sharply defined in the light reflected from the sea. He noticed that her eyes were shining like two stars. 'Like two stars,' he thought. 'Like two stars,' he said. The words took him by surprise, but he was glad that he had said them. He touched her face and caressed it gently.

'Your eyes are like my wife's,' he murmured. Katerina smiled and felt the tension dissolve between them. The breeze from the sea made her shiver. 'Let's go home,' she said.

With a kick on the pedal the captain started the engine. Once again they charged at the night which fled before them together with something else that she did not then quite grasp.

3

One afternoon they sat side by side on a rock in the shade of an aloe. All round them was the hot, sweet smell of the flowers which grew among the stones by the wells. The captain lit a cigarette and started to talk of his home; his voice was tinged with sadness.

Katerina listened. She would have liked to know something about his wife; what she was like apart from her eyes which resembled her own; if she was fair or dark, tall or short, and what she was called. He had never mentioned her name. But the captain gave her no clue. He talked about uniforms, about Italians who had been born in uniforms and about the war. He said that his generation had been born in uniform, had grown up from uniform to uniform and would die in uniform. He spoke with resignation.

'One uniform more or less, what does it matter?' said Katerina, trying to make a joke of it and to cheer him up. 'It's that which makes wars,' the captain answered. During the long silence that followed Katerina looked at him carefully. His features were not finely drawn, they were heavy and hard. She gazed at him trying to fathom the reason for his unaccustomed silence, not daring to break it. She felt an outsider and unwanted. She could not tell him that he could trust her and that he could unburden himself without shame. Wasn't the victor allowed to weep on the shoulder of the vanquished?

Perhaps he was thinking of the Anglo-American armies, advancing up Italy, marching to capture its cities, knowing that soon his own city would fall to them, exactly as had happened in Argostolion and all the towns of Greece. Perhaps he was already picturing his own wife begging for a piece of bread or a tin of meat from an American officer billeted in his house and seeing them sleeping together in his own big bed.

The captain threw away the cigarette end which was burning his fingers. He pulled himself together as though awakening from a dream. He bent his head towards Katerina.

'I am grateful to you,' he said.

'Why?' she asked.

Aldo Puglisi looked away from her. 'Because you are good.'

Katerina laughed, embarrassed. 'It is not true. How do you know I'm good?'

'We have done you great wrong,' the captain went on, almost to himself. He spoke of the girls of Argostolion, and what the victorious soldiers had done to them, and how in the long run everyone was defeated. 'Even us,' he said.

'Katerina,' said the captain, 'do you like me a little, as you might a brother?' She threw a stone and listened to the sound of the seaplane as it took off from the harbour on its reconnaissance flight. The air hung motionless over the wells.

'Soon,' she said, 'you will go home to Italy. The war is finished for you Italians. Win or lose, what does it matter? You ought to be happy.'

Aldo sighed. He tried to smile.

'You are good,' he repeated, 'you have forgiven me.'

'Forgiven you for what?' she said.

'For the harm I have done you.'

'But when did you do me any harm?' asked Katerina. She could think of nothing. Was it because of the bread and the tins left on the table, or because he had said her eyes resembled those of his wife?

One afternoon before the armistice, Karl Ritter and the captain had found themselves on the beach with the Italian girls. Karl and La Triestina had quickly become friendly and had disappeared together swimming out towards the open sea, the one chasing the other like two young dolphins at play. He and Adriana had remained together with the warmth of the still strong September sun on their skin. Gerace had been sitting on a rock some way off cursing Italian and German officers alike, gazing away towards the horizon. 'You're all the same, you officers,' he had thought half way between truth and jest, 'you always get the best women.'

Then in the distance the captain had seen Karl and La Triestina come out of the sea and run out of sight behind a clump of heather where the woods came down to the sea.

Although she had missed the point, he had said to Adriana, 'When a man takes off his uniform he sheds his ideologies. Look at Karl now: with nothing on he's just a nice boy, not a soldier of the Wehrmacht.'

He told her about Karl's strange theories and the sickness of which they were a symptom, even though outwardly he seemed like a normal man. But Adriana had looked bored and uninterested.

'He's a lovely boy,' she said.

'Yes, if only we could all live in swim suits,' he had gone on, more to himself than to Adriana, 'then there would be neither dictatorships nor wars. Just imagine our Duce haranguing the crowd in Piazza Venezia dressed only in bathing pants. Can you imagine an army of soldiers marching along in coloured trunks, with the colonels' paunches sagging, their bandy legs and the hair on their chests?'

Adriana laughed, 'I can imagine it easily,' she said.

Gerace laughed too, sitting astride a rock. 'But for the uniforms, Signor Capitano,' he said, grinning, 'we should all be equal as far as the girls are concerned.'

4

All the bells were ringing. The armistice had started. It was the evening of the eighth of September and the bells of

Argostolion sent wave after wave of clashing brazen sound out across the bay. The bells in the town were joined by the bells of the smallest and most remote villages in the hills, and their sound echoed across the mountains, down the valleys, through the olive groves and the pinewoods.

The people of the island hurried to their windows and doorways, crowded into the streets of Argostolion, Lixourion and Sami and into the alleys of the villages to find out what was happening. Katerina Pariotis looked out from her kitchen window. The girls at the villa looked out, too. They opened the shutters to see what was going on.

'It is peace,' said Signora Nina, 'Badoglio has signed the armistice.'

'Captain, shall I get our baggage ready?' asked Gerace.

The soldiers began to sing in their tents but it was rather half-hearted. It was only the bells and the islanders that were really rejoicing. Every time the voice of the announcer on the Rome Radio interrupted the programme of music to repeat the text of Marshal Badoglio's announcement, officers and men crowded round the wireless.

'Therefore,' said the voice of the announcer, 'all acts of hostility against the Anglo-American forces by the Italian armed forces must cease everywhere. They must be ready to repel any possible attack from any other quarter.'

Captain Aldo Puglisi looked at the darkening sea to the west from where at any moment until then the enemy might have come. He looked below him where to his left were the vague shapes of Franz Fauth's German battery. Through his binoculars he could see clearly the sentries who walked up and down unconcernedly as though they did not hear the joyful ringing of the bells, their machine-pistols bumping against their legs.

The announcement of the armistice did not surprise him at all. It had been expected daily since the Anglo-Americans had crossed the straits of Messina. It did not surprise him to find himself in a situation whose outcome could not be calculated.

Obviously the war was lost. Detailed reports of the Allied

advance up Italy had come from the mainland. There was nothing more that could be done. Columns of tanks, troop carriers, guns, armoured vehicles and trucks wound their way in an unending procession through the mountains of Calabria. It was said that by night they even used their headlights because the skies had been swept clear of Italian and German aircraft. Along the coast, hidden from the eyes of the Italian soldiers, was the Allied Fleet with its powerful guns trained on the enemy's positions, ready to hurl tons of explosives on to the beaches of the Tyrrhenian Sea.

They listened to these stories with amazement and as they listened they recalled their own strung out columns of pack mules climbing through the mountains of Albania, pass after pass, track after track, sometimes advancing sometimes retreating, with mules stuck in the mud of the Vojussa and left to die. Those mules had been their armoured columns!

The captain looked at the German guns and at the sentries and thought what a great joke the Duce had played on them, making them into warriors and hurling them into confusion, like the mules on the Vojussa, against an armoured enemy. He himself, he thought, had deserved it. He had believed in the legions of Caesar and in Aldo Puglisi the legionary. But as for Gerace, what harm had he done? What did he know of the race of heroes? And others like him, the artillerymen, peasants of Astigiano, Puglia and Tuscany? What fault of theirs was this squalid business? And Katerina? They had no reckoning to settle. But even though it was he who owed the debt, it was they and the like of them as well as himself who were going to have to pay it.

'Captain, shall I pack our baggage?'

Yes, the war was lost, but how could their German comrades be made to understand it? What would happen between him and his ex-messmate Karl Ritter, with whom he had been having supper night after night and with whom he had walked along the same paths in deep discussion? It seemed as if his gunners, Gerace, the chaplain and his officers, all gathered together in the big headquarters tent were asking the same question. They looked at him with diffident, perplexed smiles on their faces, with uncertainty and consternation in their eyes, mixed with happy expectation at the hope of going home again across the sea.

He would have to make Leutnant Fauth and Oberleutnant Ritter understand when he asked them for the pistols, assuring them that in exchange they and their men would be spared their lives.

'Thank you, gentlemen!' He tried to imagine the scene of the handover. He would ask them to sit down, as guests in his tent, and then he would invite them to put their pistols on the table. He would offer them a drink and they would talk about the destiny of man and about human happiness.

Gradually the ringing of the bells died away. Little by little the clangour grew less until only one bell was sounding far out in the country in the forest, and then finally that too was silent.

Night came on. The blaze of the sunset faded from the town and the mountains. The forests darkened and the sky was poised at the breaking point between day and night, with the first stars flickering faintly in it. The people of Cefalonia and the soldiers listened to the sudden silence, which although it was no different from that of any evening, seemed to hold a hidden threat. The girls at the villa saw the slender outline of a warship glide away from the harbour and make off across the bay towards the open sea. In its wake other small ships followed, minesweepers and torpedo boats, throwing out from their funnels dirty clouds of smoke against an even darker sky. It seemed as though the sea in front of the town was smouldering without flames. An acrid and cloying smell of burning coal filled the air.

Adriana shut her eyes and for a moment recalled the smells of her childhood when she used to walk in the streets near the station where steam engines were shunting in the sidings. It was only for an instant, but long enough for a thrill of pleasure to pass through her and to make her smile. For now, even for the girls, the war was finished and tomorrow she would go home and walk near the station as she used to, as if nothing at all had happened in all that time.

'What's going on?' asked Signora Nina, with a tone of reproach in her voice. Drawn by anxiety she made her way through the girls to the window to look at the ships as they sailed away.

'Look at them slinking off,' she said.

'Perhaps they are going off to attack the English,' suggested La Triestina.

The gunners on the hill, and the townspeople, saw the ships, too, in the last light of day. Leutnant Fauth and Karl Ritter saw them as they passed right under their batteries. They were like a silent flock of ducks on the motionless water of a pond, their wake spreading out behind them in a fan, scarcely visible in the gloom.

'In a few hours,' the Italian soldiers were thinking, 'they will be tying up in harbour in the south of Italy.'

And Karl Ritter thought, 'They're the same as the Greeks, an inferior people.' And he thought of the Italians and Aldo Puglisi watching the flight of their little fleet.

The captain picked up the telephone and spoke to his headquarters. There were no orders, except to keep calm and not to attack the Germans, but at the same time to be ready to repel their attack, in case they made a move. It was unlikely, thought Aldo Puglisi, because they were so thin on the ground.

The wireless, lit with blue and red valves, was giving out messages from the Allied command in Cairo and Algiers. They were asking the Italians to turn and fight the Germans, to disarm them. It was a strange sensation to hear this direct appeal from those who had been their enemies. It was as if they had awakened from one dream, only to fall at once into another. He went out, feeling the need for a breath of fresh September air, to sort out his ideas, to be alone and have a chance to think.

'They'll be going away,' thought Katerina as she looked out from her window at the mountains above Lixourion where Captain Puglisi's battery was. 'They'll be going away and then this ridiculous story will be finished.'

It was absurd, the story of her secret love, of the almost maternal tenderness for a man who had come into her home as an enemy and whom she had hated but not with her whole heart, not as she ought to have done, because she had never really succeeded in hating him. None of the Greeks had really succeeded.

'He will go away,' she thought, trying to make out the battery on the hill above the grey woods, and she sensed a feeling of relief, as though she would be freed from a burden, but at the same time she felt a pang of despair, knowing that with the inevitability of his departure, she had discovered that Cefalonia was an island, cut off from the mainland, alone and surrounded by sea on all sides.

'Do you hear anything?' asked Signora Nina. They were still all at the window, excited and happy as though they were watching a play, waiting to see something happen.

The distant sound of trotting horses came from the bridge, faint and ghostly. Then the shadow of something moving came out on to the road to Lixourion, advancing towards the cemetery.

'They're charging,' said Signora Nina in dismay.

They saw the horses coming out of the darkness. It was a cavalry patrol, the soldiers with their rifles slung on their shoulders, helmets on their heads with the straps under their chins. At the head of the patrol an officer rode, jogging up and down on his horse. The soldiers followed him, rising and falling in their saddles whilst the legs of their horses crossed to and fro on the surface of the road. The horses' manes fluttered between the glittering rifles and helmets.

'Which officer is that?' asked Signora Nina.

The patrol passed along the garden wall and the rhythm grew more pronounced. A strong smell of sweating skin and leather reached the window and entered the room.

'Soldiers, who are you?' shouted Signora Nina, leaning over the windowsill. Her voice was lost amongst the hoofbeats, but someone in the patrol had heard. 'We are Italians,' he shouted back, 'the curfew patrol.'

Horses and horsemen passed on, showing their tails and rumps. The rifle barrels flashed blue and the iron shoes on the horses' hooves struck little white and red sparks from the ground. The patrol disappeared in the direction of Lixourion and became lost in the dark but the vibration of the hooves remained in the air as though the whole island were ringing with hoofbeats from end to end.

Other squads of mounted soldiers were setting out on patrol along the paths and roads of the island. With an officer in front, rifles slung and helmet straps under their chins, the patrols went up and down along the hillsides and valleys, crossing the lifeless countryside, through meadows and deserted fields.

The photographer Pasquale Lacerba, protected by his interpreter's pass, was going home thinking about the Germans and how they ought to have captured them. He knew already that he would not get a wink of sleep that night for worrying about it all.

CHAPTER THIRTEEN

1

THE DISTANT GREY land where mists and forests joined to-gether in a sad, everlasting autumn, knew nothing of the colours of this southern world. The sea here was different from the sea up there. The coast of the Baltic was dark and storm beaten, without light or clear division between water and sky, day and night. The northern shores where only ceaseless Arctic winds beat were deserted. And his native town? He recalled the cobbled streets, the stones of the old houses, the subdued sounds of a small provincial town, the statue and the flower beds in the big square by the town hall.

He remembered that whenever he had gone beyond the old town gate he had seen fields, green, grey or black according to the time of year. Once outside the town the eye could travel far. The earth stretched away limitless and a world of nothing but plains began, with a line of telegraph poles grow-ing smaller and smaller towards the horizon and then vanish-ing. Karl used to feel on the brink of another world when he went out of the town. He used to feel alarm, almost a fear of distance and of space that used to slow his step. He would try to go on, to follow the road, he could see it now, straight as a knife blade, which would take him into the plain, but giddiness used to overcome him and drive him back to the town with its familiar buildings. There the roads had exact limits. They were bounded by doors, windows and archways. Their direction was precise, with the paved carriage ways for vehicles, street lamps, lighted or turned off, turnings and crossroads, with crowds that walked on pavements, great wagons drawn by draught horses, carts, cars and the green station bus. There life was regulated and circumscribed, not indefinite like the great plain which pressed around the town.

Since his childhood, Karl had felt that the town had been built so that men could defend themselves against the vastness of the plain, with streets, houses, and squares well laid out in geometrical patterns. And this was why his town had remained dear to him. He had been born there, of course, but, above all, because between its grey walls mellowed with time, he always felt secure.

Now on Cefalonia he was looking at the sea. He had seen seas and crossed them. He had even crossed plains. It gave him a sense of pride like passing an exam. But he had never crossed either seas or plains alone. A kind of mechanised citadel of steel came behind him or moved in front of him enabling him to overcome the sense of anxiety, of giddiness that the sight of places outside his home town gave him. He moved across the seas and plains of Europe part of an armed body, in the shelter of this multiform, nomad citadel. He wondered why, on a warm September night like this, bright with stars visible in every detail, without a trace of mist or clouds, this mood of nostalgia should have possessed him.

The army was still there and the telephone cable ran from the battery to the German headquarters in Argostolion. From there it was easy to communicate with Athens, Vienna, Berlin. In short, the citadel was performing all its functions smoothly.

He listened to the silence of the island. 'If the Italians attack us,' he thought, 'we are done for.' Three thousand grenadiers, even Germans, even of the 996th Grenadier Battalion under the command of Lieutenant Colonel Hans Barge would not have much chance against a whole division, even though it was an Italian division.

But all was quiet. The Italians were not on the move. Perhaps they were waiting for the dawn and for further orders. Perhaps they had neither the desire nor the courage to do anything. Karl Ritter smiled. 'Only good for whoremongering,' he thought. 'A race of waiters, like the Greeks.'

But the Germans, too, were waiting for the dawn. There was nothing else to do.

'We must play for time,' decided Colonel Barge.

Meanwhile from his command post in the technical school near Piazza Valianos he deployed part of his little armoured force against the possibility of an attack by the Italians. A field telephone rang and several of his ten armoured vehicles moved off on the road from Argostolion to Lixourion. Their massive squat shadows, with turrets black against the sky and their guns pointing at the stars, came clumsily out from quiet fields and olive groves with a noise of clunking tracks.

Small and weak though it was in the face of an Italian division, the German garrison functioned perfectly in every respect. The vehicles came to a halt and took up positions round an old mill with their guns covering the end of the bridge. Silence returned to the island. Karl Ritter and Captain Puglisi, Katerina, the photographer, the Italian and the German soldiers and the islanders sighed with relief: nothing was going to happen.

In the grey hall of the school Colonel Barge waited for the dawn. Through the window he saw its pale advance on the hill tops.

The Italian division commander saw it, too. All night he had been trying vainly to make wireless contact with Supergreccia, the Italian High Command in Greece, or with the government in Brindisi. Neither Supergreccia nor Italy had answered any of his many signals. And now in this new situation created by the armistice he was sure of only one thing. He knew that a head-on clash and any further bloodshed must be avoided.

He felt a sensation of horror and revulsion at the thought of blood, lives cut off in the prime of youth and his soldiers left lying in the wake of the war. His eyes red from lack of sleep gazed dazedly at the growing light of the day as it spread behind the hills. He felt the company of those young men to be strangely present at his side in the confused, bare dawn, beyond which nothing more seemed to exist. The values and traditions of centuries had crumbled. There was no government, only a king in flight; no alliances, no enemies, no allies, but only wasted blood.

The soldiers of Franz Fauth and Captain Puglisi also saw the dawn, rising up in the east, making the stars grow pale and then extinguishing them. They felt the same chill, the same indecision that marks the passage of night into day.

They started to move round the cookhouse fires. They smelt the pungent odour of boiling coffee on the cold morning air without being able to say if it came from their own stoves or from the neighbouring camp. They sipped the coffee and it cheered them after the long watch of the night. They yawned sleepily and stretched themselves to shake off the remnant of their drowsiness.

The captain got ready to go down to headquarters. All round him, with dragging feet, his men were going through their usual morning routine, towels round their necks, mess tins in their hands. They joked as they stood in front of shaving mirrors hung on poles, their faces swollen with lather. He paused to consider these movements which were going on all over the island, all over the world, just as if only on that morning of September 9th he had become aware of them. Over there, the Germans were doing the same things. Even the general, too, probably; even he would have drunk his coffee with the same momentary sensation of well being. Colonel Barge, too.

'Signor Capitano, if you'll give me a lift, I'll go down and see the old girl,' Gerace said, standing to attention in front of him, a mess tin of steaming coffee in his hand.

'Well,' thought the captain, 'not everyone is thinking the same thoughts after all.' He was glad that amongst so much similarity of action and thought there was someone like Gerace, who could think of his Greek girl. Hadn't he himself been thinking of Katerina Pariotis? He had thought of her and wanted her all night. At the same time he had thought of his wife, longing for her too; a double desire, strange and inexplicable. But in the case of Amalia it had been different, almost a duty. He had forced himself to think of her as though to free himself from a sense of guilt.

He went down to the town. He dropped Gerace outside a peasant's cottage which appeared barred and silent amongst the market gardens. He flashed by the walls of the girl's villa without slowing down – the blinds were drawn and all was still – and arrived in Piazza Valianos.

There amidst the café tables weathered by the sun, and in the offices of the Italian headquarters thick with cigarette smoke, he had watched what went on, the changing moods of that first day of peace.

Colonel Barge, wearing his best service dress uniform bright with well polished leather and buckles, drove into the piazza escorted by a squad of motorcyclists armed with machine pistols. He got out calmly at the door of the Italian head-quarters, returned the salutes of those standing round, his hand to the peak of his cap or in mid air as though the armistice had neither surprised him nor turned him against his former allies. He had come to attention before the general's desk and the door had closed behind him as heels clicked.

'Negotiations have been started,' said a voice in the crowd of officers. They had all come down into the town, junior officers and senior officers. It was like a noisy market place. Here, too, there were the same repeated gestures, the same thoughts and words multiplied again and again, projected across the piazza from café table to office desk, to the tents on the hill. Aldo Puglisi noticed that the German officers were smoking their cigarettes, too, smiling and moving restlessly around their vehicles and motorcycles, drinking and wiping away the sweat brought out by the growing heat. They too were talking and thinking and wondering about their Colonel Barge, in there in the general's office.

Presently the colonel came out, his heels echoing along the passage. In the piazza orders were shouted and engines were started up. Then rumours came out from the head-quarters with the staff officers.

'They have reached an agreement. The Germans are leaving the island tomorrow.'

'The colonel has promised to collaborate in keeping order in the island.'

'The general has invited the Germans to lunch.'

They caught a glimpse of the pale figure of the general as he got into his car. Through the closed windows his face betrayed nothing as he drove away. He would be meeting the officers of the German garrison again this time around a dinner table. Elbow to elbow with the ex-allies, he would be eating, drinking, making the usual toasts to the success of the Wehrmacht, and forcing himself to appear as if everything was quite normal but within himself he would be wondering how to resolve this incredible dilemma, feeling himself torn between the Germans and the Anglo-Americans, between Marshal Badoglio's proclamation and the physical presence of his guest, Lieutenant Colonel Hans Barge.

No, he would not want to be in the general's shoes, thought Aldo Puglisi, as he looked at the staff car driving out of the piazza with its pennant fluttering.

What if he were in the general's place? Then in the middle of the meal when eyes were glazed with eating and drinking would he not quietly give the order to seize the whole German command? He smiled at such an hospitable idea.

'Wait and see,' he said to himself. 'I'll turn out a hero yet, Aldo Puglisi the hero.' Would it not be better to go back to his camp amongst his men and dutifully await orders as he had always been taught to do? 'Go back to camp, Captain,' he said to himself, 'go back to camp and wait for orders from your superiors. They will do the thinking for you; they always have.'

But he could not tear himself away from the piazza. He had a feeling that by just being there and watching, he was doing something to help and that if he went away something would happen without him.

He also hoped that he might suddenly see Katerina Pariotis come round a corner and walk across the square. If nothing had happened he would have gone to see her in the evening and they would have ridden down to the lighthouse and the sea mills on his motorcycle.

But towards the evening the order came from Supergreccia. It burst amongst the café tables in the piazza, and spread round the units and the soldiers. Everyone knew it. XI Army Headquarters had sent a radiogram from Athens signed by General Vecchiarelli, in which the Acqui Division was ordered to lay down its arms to the Germans.

CHAPTER FOURTEEN

1

THE JUNKERS FLEW over Lixourion and Argostolion. The great black transport planes circled and landed on the mirror-like water off Lixourion. Colonel Barge was receiving reinforcements. It was the morning of September 10th.

'Are we really going to lay down our arms?' Captain Puglisi wondered. He watched the flight of the Junkers and glanced at the mountainous backbone of the island. He directed his binoculars on to the streets and roofs of Argostolion. The field telephone had just informed unit commanders that the colonel had presented himself to the general and had demanded the surrender of the division.

'He demanded that the division lay down their arms tomorrow at eleven o'clock in Piazza Valianos.'

The captain listened to the voices of his soldiers on the hill. They spoke of Supergreccia, and of Badoglio's government. They said that there was still time to attack the Germans. He heard the roar of the aeroplanes in the sky and the sound of the German trucks and motorcycles moving about the island. There was an unaccustomed activity on the dusty roads of Cefalonia.

'Are we really going to hand over our arms, drawn up like a parade, in Piazzo Valianos, tomorrow at eleven?' he kept asking himself.

He did not want to think about it. The war was over. Soon they would have returned home and would have taken up life where they had left off all those years ago.

The voices and sounds on the hill around him brought to mind the voices and sounds of home and the face and eyes of

Amalia. He thought of his son. How many times had he seen him since he was born? It was strange about Amalia's voice. He could conjure up every detail of her face, lovely but a little expressionless, but he could not succeed in recalling the sound of her voice.

This inability to remember Amalia's voice made him angry. He tried desperately to recreate it. It was a voice that was both delicate and strong, capable of expressions of tenderness. Each time he thought he had found it, he realized with despair that it was not his wife's voice, but Katerina's.

By an effort of memory, he held his wife's face in his mind's eye and saw again the country lanes in the plain of Lombardy by the walls of an old farmhouse where he used to take Amalia when she had been his girl. At the same time he could see the road into Argostolion along which little cars, glittering like tin toys, their windscreens flashing, were making their way towards the town. He recalled their conversation, beneath the ivy covered walls, but even then he could not recall Amalia's voice. He could only conjure up a voiceless Amalia, or one who spoke with the voice of Katerina. Mixed with all this he heard the voices of his officers, one of whom was talking about the orders from headquarters which had come by telephone.

'The general has called all the senior officers of the division to a meeting. He wants to discuss Colonel Barge's demands with them.'

'Are we really going to surrender?' the captain asked himself again.

'Unit commanders are not to leave their posts.'

The captain looked through his binoculars at the headquarters amongst the houses of Argostolion piled one on top of the other. He felt he could almost see the general seated at his desk listening to the opinions of his senior officers as he stared at the sheet of paper which lay on his desk top between his limp hands. He could almost read the words which were written there. It was the order from Supergreccia to hand over their arms to Colonel Barge.

He raised his glasses to the Junkers which continued to

pass over the mouths of the guns. He thought that once again, someone else was deciding the division's fate, the fate of Captain Aldo Puglisi, and that it was far from agreeable to him to leave the decision to the general and his senior officers gathered together in council.

But what would their decision be? he wondered.

Then the tiny vehicles started to leave Argostolion and travel the island roads in the opposite direction, carrying the senior officers back to their commands. The field telephone rang and the impersonal voice of the telephonist was heard. 'All the senior officers, except two, have declared themselves in favour of the surrender.'

'Tomorrow at eleven o'clock in Piazza Valianos,' Captain Aldo Puglisi repeated mechanically. To escape the incredulous eyes of Gerace and his officers and men and so as not to have to answer their questions he went some way from the tent and sat down under an olive tree. From there he could see the peninsula of Argostolion as far as Capo San Teodoro and a vast tract of the Ionian Sea.

Was this the right decision? wondered Aldo Puglisi.

The Badoglio Government had ordered them to keep their arms and to defend themselves against any enemy attack. The division could not only defend itself, but in the space of a few hours could disarm the grenadiers of Hans Barge. Why then had the decision to surrender been made? Because someone would rather obey the orders of Supergreccia than the orders of the legitimate government? He got to his feet as though to escape from having to give himself an answer.

The soldiers were talking loudly. They spoke of ten thousand against three thousand. They said that the Germans would have been taken prisoner without firing a shot if only the general and the senior officers had obeyed the government. They kept asking the same question, why should we surrender?

'So that we can go home,' someone replied. 'If we lay down our arms, the Germans will let us go home.' But a chorus of protest swamped the reply. No one believed that once they had parted with their arms the Germans would let them go.

Aldo Puglisi asked if they all wanted to be courtmartialled. Then the voices died down and there was silence on the hill. The sound of the vehicles and the roar of the planes was heard more clearly, but as soon as he turned to go back to the olive tree, the voices started up again.

Leaning against the tree trunk, his memory went back to the wall round the old farm and he hardly heard the sound of the voices so different from the voices of Katerina and Amalia. After so many uniforms, the only thing that now mattered was for him to take off his uniform for ever, to return home, to walk along the streets of his home town again with Amalia on his arm and to get acquainted with his unknown son. Let him leave Cefalonia to its people, and Greece and all the other places that he had marched through to their people. Let him leave Katerina Pariotis to her own fate.

This was the important thing for him, not the rounding up of the German garrison, the supremacy of the division over the grenadiers, of the general over the lieutenant colonel. He dreamed of embarking on a ship, any ship, and setting course for Italian seas. It did not matter to him whether he was armed or disarmed. Listening to the voices of his men all round him, it seemed to him that this was their feeling too. It was only for this, with the object of getting home, that they were discussing whether to disarm the Germans or surrender their arms to the Germans.

He got up and focused his binoculars on the main road to Kardakata. 'Captain, look down there,' someone cried. A column of soldiers and vehicles were moving along the road. The 3rd Battalion of the 317th Infantry Regiment were coming down the valley towards Argostolion. What was happening? they asked. Why had the battalion abandoned such an important strategic point?

'They are coming down to surrender,' cried the gunners. 'We'll get the same order. We'll have to go down there to Piazza Valianos.'

'Yes, perhaps we will,' thought the captain. They had started the operation of moving into the city to lay down their arms.

Behind him Gerace was speaking. 'The general has ordered the evacuation of Kardakata.'

'The general is betraying us,' someone shouted.

2

The general watched the movements of his troops as they abandoned their position at Kardakata. He saw the evening shadows creeping down the hills and growing longer across the road to the Lixourion peninsula, whilst on the other side of the bay the waters began to darken. It was the third night since the Italian government had announced the armistice and the general knew that it would be his third night without sleep.

He sat at his desk. There was a photograph of his wife by the telephone amidst a litter of papers. In front of him typed out in capital letters with General Vecchiarelli's signature at the foot was the text of the wireless signal from Supergreccia.

It was an incredible message with an incredible signature.

Once again, he turned over in his mind the strange coincidence between the wireless signal from General Vecchiarelli and the unexpected demand for surrender from the German colonel. He felt a premonition that during the outwardly peaceful night a secret conspiracy was growing around him, the island, and the division. He felt the presence of someone who from afar off was preparing to cast a net and the net was going to fall around Cefalonia.

How could the net be broken? By surrendering their arms in Piazza Valianos tomorrow?

The strategic point at Kardakata had already been abandoned, so that, according to the general's thinking, Colonel Barge would have no fears concerning the Italians' good intentions. Kardakata was vital to the defence of the island, and to give it up was concrete testimony of not wanting to make a fight of it.

Would this be enough for the colonel, or would he insist, in accordance with the orders of Supergreccia, on the surrender of arms in Piazza Valianos? If, as he had maintained, it was his wish that the division should return to Italy, what was the point in insisting on the surrender of arms?

The general walked to the window. It was dark. The sea and the night met without division. The harbour was empty. He heard the beat of horses' hooves from the town. It was the patrol and the sound echoed through the alleys and streets. The division was sleeping out there in front of him, in their billets, in their camps, at their gun sites, and in the barracks.

He heard again the voices of his senior officers giving their views on the German demand for surrender. All except two of them had been in agreement. But supposing the Germans did not keep their side of the bargain and the two officers who had been against the surrender were right and that they ought to move against the Germans at once to forestall their probable attack, thereby obeying the orders of the government and ignoring the signal from Supergreccia?

Alone with his conscience he saw the whole situation clearly. The division could have easily won the first battle against the Germans, but it would have been destroyed by the Luftwaffe because the Italian air force was locked up on the southern front and no help could have been expected from the Navy. They would have had to stay where they were on that tongue of land poised between sea and sky, awaiting the vengeance which would not have been long in coming.

The vengeance of the Stukas, thought the general, looking up at the sky. It was still and bright with stars and there was no sound of Junkers. It was a calm, quiet night well suited to reflection and to plotting. In distant cities on the mainland, someone was busy weaving a plot; he felt sure of it; in Athens, Berlin, or Brindisi. Why did the fugitive government not reply to his appeals? Did they want to leave the whole weight of responsibility for the choice between surrender and battle to him alone?

Yes, it was a propitious night for great decisions. Supported by the majority of his senior officers he had made up his mind. But what if the Germans failed to honour the agreement and took the whole division prisoner? What was he going to say to his soldiers then?

And now just as soon as he had finally reached a decision, the problem started to repeat itself all over again.

To obey the King or Supergreccia?

To surrender their weapons tomorrow morning in a few hours in Piazza Valianos or to refuse the colonel's demands, fight it out and spill more blood?

3

The general's indecision was to continue until the moment of his death.

All through the night of the 10th Captain Puglisi and the other unit commanders waited for the field telephone to bring them the order to march down to Piazza Valianos. But in the tents, barracks and gun posts the telephones were silent and the night passed.

Colonel Barge had been waiting, too, for the official acceptance of his demand for the surrender, but he had received no message.

The sun was already high in the sky and eleven o'clock was not far off. The face of the clock in his office in the technical school showed 9.40. He walked up and down the restricted space of the room with his hands behind his back, looking now at the clock and now at the sky. The regular flights of the Junkers had started again and they continued to unload supplies of arms and ammunition off the shore at Lixourion. But reinforcements of men, where were they?

Hans Barge stood still. He knew for a certainty that if the Italians made a move before his first reinforcements arrived, his men would be overcome. But, he knew with equal certainty, that the Wehrmacht would not give up the Ionian Islands and that from the airfields of Albania and Greece they would send up clouds of Stukas whose support would turn the battle in his favour. Only one thing surprised him and that was how the Italian general could fail to understand the situation and how he could persist in putting off an inevitable decision.

He possessed himself in patience for a minute, a quarter of an hour, an hour, in the hope that the Italian general would realize the inevitability of his fate. He gave him a little longer, still hoping that he might be saved the unpleasant task of having to deliver the ultimatum which had just arrived from general headquarters. Berlin had transmitted questions which the colonel was to submit to the Italian divisional commander: was he with or against the Germans? was he going to give up his weapons? The general was not to be allowed more than eight hours to reach his decision.

A good, realistic commander, thought the colonel, would have found eight minutes long enough to make the right decision. If he had had enough men he would have helped the general out of his dilemma.

He buttoned his tunic, ran quickly down the stairs and jumped into his car. Followed by his escort he was driven to the Italian headquarters and he presented himself once again to the general.

'General,' he said, standing by his desk, 'up till now I have received no message from you about the acceptance or rejection of my offer concerning the surrender. Therefore I have been authorized to consider it to have been refused.'

The general asked the colonel to sit down. A soldier brought up a chair to the desk but Hans Barge declined it.

'General,' he went on, 'I do not know for what motives you have rejected my offer for the surrender which should have taken place this morning at eleven o'clock in Piazza Valianos. But now I have the honour to submit for your attention the demands just sent to me by signal from my government. It is for you, General, to decide the future of our association on the island. You have eight hours to decide.'

Colonel Barge had finished. His glance fell on a photograph of a woman which stood beside the telephone. Then he raised his eyes to a crucifix hanging by itself on the white wall behind the desk. He could not leave at once as he had wanted to because the general started to explain the reasons for his delay. The colonel did not pay much attention to them because he was convinced that they were senseless. No reasons could be sufficiently plausible to explain such behaviour as the general's.

'I have thought about it at great length,' he heard the general say. 'I cannot accept your demand for the surrender without a written guarantee of the freedom of movement of the division. I demand written guarantees that the whole division will be repatriated.'

'You have,' interrupted the colonel, 'eight hours to make your final decision. As to written guarantees, I will ask my government.'

The general sat motionless after the German had left the office. With his arms stretched out before him on the desk, he gazed into space, beyond the photograph of his wife, beyond the empty chair, beyond the window. Mechanically he had picked up the piece of paper which the colonel had left and tested its thickness between the tips of his fingers. It was the Wehrmacht's ultimatum, presented according to the rules of the game.

Would they respect the surrender terms? Would they agree to give written guarantees?

His conviction that he had acted wisely in postponing the surrender grew. He had gained time for the division and now he would be able to listen to the advice of his army chaplains.

He felt worn out by the waiting and his inner conflict, but reassured. He picked up the telephone and gave the order for the chaplains to come to his headquarters. There were only eight hours in which to arrive at a definite decision. Eight hours in which to answer many questions, including those put by his own conscience.

The chaplains came in from their units. They were for neither helping nor attacking the Germans. As the senior officers had been the day before they were in favour of surrendering the weapons against written guarantees. Only one of them declared himself against the surrender.

The general looked from one to another in silence, thanking them without speaking. He had watched them as he listened to their words and a comforting feeling of calm had come over him dispelling the rest of his weariness. His own feelings he now knew to be shared by his senior officers, and his chaplains, and therefore by his soldiers. The division was with him, sharing his fears, his uncertainties, and his desire to avoid further bloodshed.

The chaplains went back to their units taking with them the good news of a settlement which would certainly be reached with firm guarantees. The soldiers wanted to believe in it, to force themselves to think it was true and that the German colonel would write down and sign the guarantees for the surrender.

'Boys, we'll soon be home,' someone said. But others asked if they could trust the Germans, even if they had signed a piece of paper, and the moment of euphoria passed.

Captain Puglisi wondered about it too, as he waited all day for orders.

The answer came in the early hours of the evening. Unexpectedly news came from the neighbouring island of Santa Maura that after the Italian garrison had laid down their arms, they had all been made prisoners and that their commanding officer, Colonel Ottalevi, had been shot.

CHAPTER FIFTEEN

1

WHEN THE EIGHT hours had elapsed, the general did not order his division to surrender their arms. By radio, from Brindisi, he had received instructions to resist the Germans. By sea, from Santa Maura, had come confirmation of their treachery.

He gave no orders for surrender but neither did he order an attack on the Germans. He went on hoping that in spite of everything there could be an agreed settlement which would allow the Italians to keep their arms.

Nor had Colonel Barge made any move. He had not yet sufficient troops at his disposal, but he wanted to give the Italians an example of what might be in store for them. He chose a suitable point and Oberleutnant Ritter the instrument.

As the first stars of evening came out, Karl Ritter appeared in front of the Italian artillery position. He did not enter it. He shouted for Captain Puglisi and Gerace ran to warn him. He had seen the shadows of German soldiers outside the camp, he said. Aldo Puglisi rose to his feet in the grip of a feeling for which he was unprepared. He lit a cigarette, trying unsuccessfully to hide the trembling of his hands from his men. But he was not really afraid, he was embarrassed, almost ashamed, as if the order for the armistice with the Anglo-Americans and the renunciation of the war on the part of the Italians was his work, as if he personally had betrayed Karl.

'Don't go, Captain,' Gerace said, 'it will be the same here as on Santa Maura.' Like Santa Maura, he thought, as he buckled on his pistol, and he saw again the island, tiny in the quiet, blue waters of the Ionian, as he had seen it on the cross-

104

ing that day when they had landed in the archipelago. He saw too, in a flash, but precise in every detail, the Italian colonel, his back to a wall, and a firing squad aiming their machine pistols at him.

'You must reach an understanding,' the chaplain said, hurrying up beside him. Don Mario looked at him with his bright blue eyes, small in his long thin face. Nervously he twisted his hands which protruded from the too long sleeves of his tunic. He looked at him with pleading in his eyes as though to remind him of what the general had laid down, that nothing rash was to be done and as though the outcome of the armistice depended on the captain.

'So much has happened already,' Aldo Puglisi said as he walked along the path. 'Who can put off the inevitable now?' Not one of them could stop the course of events. They were in the midst of something far bigger than themselves. Unexpectedly they found themselves on a stage to play an unrehearsed part. And now the play was in full swing and it had gone wrong, against their will. But had they ever had any will? Perhaps this was the first time since he had put on a uniform that he would have been able to do something in his own way. Was it too late?

He knew himself to lack the stuff of heroes and to be unable to do anything on his own, but even now when he found himself alone under the open sky, and saw the boundary of the Italian camp against the horizon, he did not feel afraid. Karl Ritter was there waiting for him at the other end of the path, just as though it were a duel in the olden days, but all he could feel was embarrassment and shame as though he were really guilty of something.

Guilty of wanting to put an end to a war that was already lost?

They walked along the well beaten track in silence. Behind him were the chaplain, Gerace and some of his officers. As they went along they were joined by more of his officers and men, following one behind the other, each one keeping his own silence.

The sea stretched away between the almost invisible arms

of the bay. Somewhere down there after his absence of a few days which seemed an eternity, perhaps Katerina was thinking about him and the captain smiled against his will. He would have liked her to see him, her conquering captain, the uninvited lodger, the brother, on his way to the reckoning with his ex-comrade Karl Ritter.

The oberleutnant stood at the edge of the field with the empty night behind him. Along the boundary of the camp the shadows of German soldiers loomed. He could see in the darkness that they held their machine pistols at the ready. He saw the white of their hands against the dark metal of their weapons. Karl Ritter looked at him indifferently without recognition as though it was the first time they had met. Nonetheless the captain could not but recall their last meeting by the sea with the girls from the villa.

'If only there were no more uniforms,' thought Aldo Puglisi, looking at Karl's camouflage tunic.

He was wearing it in a very purposeful manner and he, too, was holding his machine pistol at the ready. His two hands were clamped on the butt, while his gaze moved from the captain to the men behind him and then took in the whole extent of the camp as though he was working out its possible resistance.

'I have orders to collaborate with you, Signor Capitano,' he said in his clear precise Italian. 'Why don't you come in, Karl?' replied Aldo Puglisi. Karl smiled, or went through the process of smiling, so it seemed to the captain in the faint light of the stars.

'Signor Capitano,' Karl went on, 'as I am sure that you will agree, our relationship has taken an unexpected turn. Certain precautions are necessary before I cross your threshold.'

Shifting his weight from foot to foot, he awaited a reply with his gun clasped to his chest. His steady gaze met and held that of the captain.

'I can understand your hesitation in answering me, Signor Capitano,' Karl said slowly, continuing to look at him.

Aldo Puglisi threw his cigarette into the dust of the pathway which widened out into a flat space where they had

106

stopped. He felt the presence of his men behind him. The chaplain and Gerace were beside him, like two guardian angels. The oberleutnant's gaze took them in too. He seemed amused at their presence.

'What sort of collaboration had you in mind, Signor Oberleutnant?' asked the captain.

Karl Ritter shifted his weight, and turned his head towards his men whose shadows around the entrance to the camp had become darker in the night.

'Signor Capitano,' said Karl, addressing him directly, 'keep calm, there is no question of fighting. I am simply carrying out the orders which have been transmitted to me from my high command. You too will carry out the orders which you have been given, isn't that so?'

The captain bowed his head in agreement.

'I have orders,' said Karl, 'to make you hand over your arms, Signor Capitano, yours and those of your battery. And you have orders from your command to offer no resistance.'

'From what command?' asked Aldo Puglisi. But he knew the reply before he had spoken.

'You know better than I do,' replied Karl Ritter with firmness. 'From your army command.'

As though accidentally, he had moved the barrel of his weapon in the captain's direction and looked him up and down from head to foot. 'Please surrender your revolver to me, Signor Capitano, and would you be so good as to pass on the orders of the Third Reich to your men,' he said.

'Do what he says,' said Don Mario.

Ritter pointed his pistol at the chaplain and moved it in a semi-circle covering Gerace and the men standing behind the captain. At the same time he shouted an order into the night and the shadows of the German soldiers became taller against the empty sky, whilst the metallic sound of safety catches being pushed forward was heard.

'Beautifully staged,' said Aldo Puglisi.

'I promise you that we have no intention of just play-acting,' said the oberleutnant with a smile.

'I can well believe it,' retorted the captain wearily. 'Am I

107

going to be shot, too, like Colonel Ottalevi?'

'I do not know anything about that,' said Karl Ritter.

It did not really matter to Aldo Puglisi what fate had in store for him. He felt as though his destiny had already been fulfilled and that he was watching himself from above. He unfastened his revolver and threw it at Karl's feet; not as a gesture of despair but of weariness. He turned to find one of his officers to pass on the order to the battery to leave their guns and lay down their rifles. All round him he saw sad, bewildered faces.

'Are you worrying about our lost military honour?' he would have liked to have said to them. 'But how can there be honour when a Marshal of Italy has run away and even a king has fled in the night like a chicken thief?'

'You,' he wanted to shout at his officers, 'what would you have done in my place, surrounded as we are? Don't you see them all round us, that they have surrounded us? Would you put up a fight?'

The officers unbuckled their belts and dropped their revolvers to the ground in silence. He would have liked to have explained to them that he was only obeying the orders of the high command of the XI Army, no more, no less, exactly as Karl Ritter had stated. Had they forgotten the existence of the signal bearing the signature of General Vecchiarelli?

He smiled at Karl. The young warrior with the twisted mind stood in front of him with his legs apart, wearing his combat suit as a bride might wear her wedding dress, his cartridge belt slung round him and his machine pistol clasped in his fists. The conqueror of the world was looking at him. Who could have imagined that only a few days before on a sunny afternoon he had been thrashing the sea in pursuit of the naked body of a whore, like any other earthy man?

'What will happen when we have surrendered our weapons?' Aldo asked. Karl laughed. 'Have no fear,' he replied, 'you will go back to your headquarters in Argostolion.' He was encouraging them sarcastically not to be frightened, but now that the first embarrassing moments were past the captain felt completely at his ease, as relaxed as ever he had felt in his life. Something was now behind him, between him and the uniforms, the excuses of expediency, prestige and military alliances. Now that he was at the mercy of Ritter's pistol he was free to choose for himself and to make his own alliances.

His men came on to the open space like a herd of sheep and stopped in a ragged mob behind their captain, hesitating in the darkness, their eyes glittering, and kicking up an acrid smell of dust into the night air.

The German soldiers came slowly forward, Karl rapped out an order. The Italians had to stretch their arms up towards the stars. Then by the light of electric torches German hands frisked over them in a search for concealed weapons. An Italian soldier swore, others wept openly like children grown afraid, others declared that they would all be shot like the colonel of Santa Maura. The chaplain knelt on the ground praying in a loud voice.

The captain shouted out, 'It's all right, don't panic, we're being sent down to the town.'

Then there was silence. Oberleutnant Ritter and his men had finished their search and they drew back to allow the Italian soldiers to pass through them without letting them out of sight. They formed a funnel of camouflage tunics and machine pistols.

'Forward, men,' Aldo Puglisi shouted, avoiding the face of Karl Ritter, and led the way through the shadowy group of German soldiers. He expected that at any moment the chatter of machine pistols would start behind him and spurts of flame would burst out into the blackness of the night. He felt as though he were walking suspended between earth and sky.

But instead the Germans let them go. They let them go down towards the plain. They went down silently without their arms.

2

Signora Nina heard the confused sound of their footsteps beyond the garden wall. It was the fourth night that she had been unable to sleep. She heard them walking and talking on the road as though they were coming that way quite casually. 'Customers,' she thought, and not withstanding the exhaustion of sleepless nights she felt pleased and even elated, because customers meant a return to normal.

She went to the window without turning on the light and looked down through the shutter. Outside the night was bright and clear. She saw them coming along in a disorderly mass, swaying across the road, some with lighted cigarettes, some with their hands in their pockets and others with their hands swinging dejectedly at their side.

They passed along the wall and reappeared in the open still huddled together like a flock of sheep. They went towards the bridge to Argostolion. They were Italian soldiers, but why were they walking? wondered Signora Nina.

Many of them had looked towards the villa, but not one of them had shown any sign of coming in. Signora Nina had heard a confused babble of talking and some laughter that had died as soon as it had started.

'Why don't you stop?' she had wanted to shout out. 'How can you pass by without stopping?'

Fearfully she had opened the shutters and had leant out to see them disappearing into the distance. Her diaphanous dressing-gown had fluttered round her slender body, thin and dry as a stick. She felt small and afraid at the sight of the soldiers going away and then weak and defeated. With the girls asleep in their rooms and the soldiers vanishing into the night she felt helpless and abandoned, just a weak woman. They were all of them poor, abandoned women, betrayed by their own protectors for whom they had risked their necks a thousand times and for whom they were still risking them.

'The ingratitude of mankind,' she thought, almost happy at having fresh proof if it.

Tomorrow she would go and seek out Agostino Sabados, the skipper of a caique, and bargain with him for the rescue of her girls. She felt herself to be their saviour and the idea moved her to tears. Softened by her own goodness, filled with self pity at the thought of her lot, she wept.

110

She saw herself for ever on the world's roads, in perpetual flight from something, perpetually searching for some new haven. She saw herself on the deck of a caique, with her girls stretched round her prostrated by the wind and sea, their hair awry, plastered on their faces, their eyes wide open with fear.

3

The passing of danger is followed by an unexpected elation and all that has happened seen in perspective seems incredible. Once again he savoured the goodness of being alive. He heard again the silence of the island, the sound of running water and the wind moving in the pine trees. He noted things that he had never seen before his brush with death, a little stream babbling down the mountainside, a wooden bridge that he must have crossed a thousand times, even flowers in the gardens, the brightness of the starlight against the intense black of the night sky, the sound of a hooter from a cargo boat moored in the bay.

Aldo Puglisi felt overwhelmed by the recollection of what had just taken place and by the sensation of things rediscovered or seen for the first time. He held Katerina's hands in his with wonder. They were both strange and familiar hands. They were Katerina's but Amalia's too; a past and a present allowed him by death. And when he took Katerina in his arms it was not only because he loved her but because he loved his wife.

At the moment when Katerina gave herself to him with a happiness equal to his own, smiling at him with surprise equal to his, he felt that death no longer existed and was no longer possible. He had seen it face to face and overcome it, escaping from it unhurt. And there he was in Katerina Pariotis' garden, with Katerina and Amalia in his arms and a desire to live and to love that could never be extinguished.

'Little Kyria,' he said. Aldo Puglisi and Katerina looked

at each other in the cold white light of dawn. This was the fourth or fifth dawn that he had seen break. But that morning the daybreak seemed different, more full of promise, lit by a new light, intense and sparkling like Katerina's eyes.

'What has been happening?' Katerina asked as she freed herself from his arms. Happiness was over. In the clear light of early day she saw for the first time Captain Puglisi before her not in the uniform of the conqueror but of the defeated.

It was not from his unbuttoned jacket, from his uniform that no longer seemed a uniform, nor from the beard which darkened his cheeks, nor from the unaccustomed hour at which he had called on her, that she knew it, but from his expression of having just rediscovered life and escaped from death.

She felt that he was now one of the family, one of her own blood. Happy for a fleeting moment, but defenceless, too, like a Greek of Cefalonia. No longer was he the lodger, the friend, but something closer, irrevocably tied.

Now he was as a brother or a father or even a son. He could never be anything else.

She took him into the house and made him sit on the side of the bed in her room which he knew so well as it was the room he had rented. She spoke to him softly as though he were a child. She helped him undress and get himself into bed and told him not to be frightened while she went into the kitchen to make him a cup of coffee.

He smiled at the motherly tone of Katerina's voice as she spoke of coffee, told him to take a little nap, and to shut his eyes, just like a baby. From the kitchen she told him not to worry. Before the sun was up she would be able to go down to the town to find out what was happening, and if things were going badly she could come back and take care of him. How long was it, asked the voice of Katerina, since he had slept?

Aldo Puglisi thought vaguely of the nights and the desolate dawns. But now his horizons were limited to the walls of this, his home, and he thought he heard Katerina's voice and Amalia's voice speaking to him from them. Then finally the welcome smell of coffee reached him and transformed itself

112

into a sense of physical and mental well being.

'Here you are, Captain,' a voice was saying, and from then on a thick curtain cut across his memory.

4

In the full light of day Colonel Barge's troops were openly taking up good strategic positions. Ten Tiger tanks were covering the road to Argostolion. They took up position amongst the green of the eucalyptus trees at the beginning of the avenue. Their engines were still. The turrets turned slowly until the guns pointed towards Piazza Valianos. The crews jumped down. Some lit cigarettes, others took off the muzzle caps of the lowered barrels and watched with sleepy eyes the emptiness of the road, disturbed only by one small figure.

Katerina passed in front of the row of tanks which seemed like great weary prehistoric beasts with armoured hide giving off their natural odour of petrol and oil. She felt that they were alive, motionless but cunning, ready to spring. She tried to walk by naturally, but she felt selfconscious with her eyes fixed in front of her and aware that the movements of her body seemed slow and her legs heavy.

The Germans looked at her as she hurried determinedly by. She seemed small in her thin red dress, even smaller seen from above from the turrets or from behind the tank tracks. They watched her without saying anything. To them she was just a colourful apparition, unimportant, having no connection with the task they had in hand.

Soon they lost interest in her and started talking again, taking up their discussion which for a moment they had broken off. Were their ex-allies really capable of turning on them, of committing the final betrayal? Had they really the courage for it? On the other hand mightn't it be better, too, if they, the Germans, finished with the war once and for all?

Katerina heard sounds rather than words. They were sharp

guttural sounds, not shouted out, but expressed quietly, as people might speak in the shadowy nave of a church. Not one of the Germans had taken much notice of her, and Katerina felt their indifference, the warriors' detachment. Nonetheless, she hurried her pace fearfully, eager to be past the last tank and to come out into Piazza Valianos, away from the stench of petrol and metal, the repellent sweat of those great mechanical beasts.

She left them behind and arrived in the piazza, in the fresh air away from the smells except the familiar smell of the sea and the hills. She felt calmer and slowed her footsteps. The awnings of the cafés had already been stretched across the pavements. The tables and chairs were outside in neat rows ready for customers. But who would come to drink ouzo or raki that morning? She saw Nicolino through the glass door. He was cleaning the counter with his usual long patient strokes across the marble slab. In the piazza, now that the tanks had shut off their engines, there was silence. Perhaps nothing had happened and nothing would happen.

She heard the hooves of a horse. She turned and crossed the piazza in the direction of Via Principe di Piemonte, the main street where she knew the Italian and German head-quarters to be, looking around her and listening. The hooves came nearer. They came from an alley leading from the sea at right angles to the square. A horse's head came round the corner followed by Matias seated up on his box and behind him in the black dusty carriage, filling it to overflowing, were the old Italian lady and her girls, painted and peroxided, around her.

The carriage stopped by the pavement near Nicolino's café. It creaked on its high wheels whilst Matias sat motionless on the box and the horse looked on sadly from between the shafts. Signora Nina and the girls got down like a flight of birds, they swarmed amongst the chairs and tables and seated themselves in a fluttering of colour and eyes, of bare arms and legs. But this time there was no one to watch the scene except Katerina Pariotis across the square, who looked behind her as she hurried away down the Via Principe di Piemonte.

A dispatch rider on a motorcycle passed and then an Italian staff car with pennants fluttering. Overhead a solitary aeroplane with the white and black cross painted on its wings and body crossed the city and the bay.

'Nicolino,' called Signora Nina. 'Nicolino.'

Colonel Barge's car went past escorted by German motorcyclists.

Signora Nina could not keep still that morning. She got up, went through the glass door and met Nicolino in the middle of the room as he ran to take her orders. She took him by the arm and led him over to the counter and asked him in a whisper that the girls could not hear if he knew where to find Agostino Sabados, the caique skipper, and if that good man would be disposed to take them on board his ship. It was up to Nicolino to persuade him, Signora Nina reminded him, otherwise he would get no cut on the deal.

She drew breath and waited. Her glittering eyes were glassy and red-rimmed from lack of sleep.

Nicolino looked out of the window into the piazza. He saw Colonel Barge get out of his car beyond the palm trees and make his way rapidly towards the Italian headquarters. His escort had drawn up around him. His soldiers, in combat dress, with their machine pistols hanging on their chests from leather straps, remained motionless outside, guarding the car whilst the colonel, followed by his officers, disappeared into the shadow of the doorway.

Nicolino thought things were going badly and that they had gone too far by a long way. Signora Nina's red-rimmed eyes and her pleading voice confirmed it. He replied mechanically that as soon as Agostino Sabados returned he would speak to him, but to Signora Nina's pressing questions as to from where he was returning Nicolino did not know how to reply.

He looked around him uncertainly, at the deserted room, bright with marble and bottles, at the wooden shelves against the wall, at the hissing coffee machine. It was a look that travelled beyond the walls of the room and the piazza and took in the sea and the mountain, and Cefalonia and the world, and also nothing at all. Signora Nina felt frightened. She forced her lips into a smile, but there was a cold fear inside her, in her mouth and in her eyes, and it constricted the muscles of her stomach. She smiled as she went out with Nicolino and sat down between Adriana and La Triestina. After they had given their orders she managed to say, 'Keep calm, girls. The skipper is ready to take us aboard should it prove necessary.'

'How many drachmae?' asked La Triestina without interest. To her Cefalonia or Italy made no difference. It was always a miserable existence. She looked amongst the Germans in the escort in the hope of seeing her fair-haired Karl Ritter. She had lost sight of him since the afternoon on the beach. But even his face was dull and uninteresting. When all was said and done what difference was there between Karl Ritter and an Italian soldier or even any civilian?

'Three thousand,' lied Signora Nina.

Adriana looked at her closely, sharply almost, with unnecessary attention, and she understood that Adriana knew and that she was caught out in a barefaced lie.

'Three thousand drachmae,' Signora Nina repeated weakly as though to challenge her.

Now people were crossing the square. Women, old men, the children of Argostolion and unemployed Cefaliots, faded and colourless in their clothes threadbare from the misery of the times and from the war. Their faces were marked by gnawing hunger which the tins and loaves of the division had not been able to satisfy. The Karamelli sisters passed slowly by as though on the prowl for clients. They had a certain air of superiority now that they were well in with the Germans or so it seemed to Nicolino as he put the glasses down in front of the girls.

'Viva Badoglio, Nicolino!' said La Triestina distractedly. 'Viva,' he replied under his breath lest the Germans should hear. But today La Triestina did not even smile. She looked out at the throng in the piazza which now included Italian soldiers and officers. They and their vehicles, motorcycles and lorries were going to and fro along the Via Principe di Piemonte. Unit commanders and staff officers came in and out of the headquarters. Only the Germans did not move. They waited patiently in silence for their colonel who in the general's office was trying once more to persuade his ex-ally to lay down his arms and retire from the battle.

Like fighters in formation, a flight of gulls appeared in the sky above the piazza. They wheeled to the left towards the sea, passing over the roofs that lined the road to the port.

At exactly that moment, the crisp crack of revolver shots was heard. They came from the direction of the naval head-quarters on the mole. They echoed faintly round Piazza Valianos and were lost in its space. The Italian soldiers and officers turned to look as did the girls and Signora Nina, Nicolino, and all the people in the piazza. The German escort looked, too.

The shots were heard in the Via Principe di Piemonte. Katerina stopped in her tracks and like everyone else looked round and wondered what had happened.

'What is it?' asked Signora Nina.

Matias woke up and scratched his head. The horse between the shafts woke up, too. It blew itself out with a great sigh which showed its bones through its skin.

'Well,' sighed Signora Nina, drained of all energy. 'Well what, Signora Nina?' asked Adriana, looking at her ironically and crossly as though it was all her fault.

From the street to the sea, groups of Italian soldiers started to appear. They were shouting and waving their hands in the bright sunlight. They were in disorder, their faces red with excitement. An officer was running with them, now at their head, now at their side, his arms raised like some ridiculous orchestral conductor, as if he wanted to silence them, or halt them, or turn them away.

'They have killed a captain,' someone cried in the middle of the piazza. 'A sergeant-major has shot his captain.'

The piazza started to empty as though in front of a strange gust of wind. The German soldiers moved closer together, their guns at the ready, back to back round their colonel's car. Carabinieri and military police hurried into the piazza. They seemed to pause and look around in search of some obstacle to overcome, some mass to break up. Then they directed themselves towards the soldiers and the officer who still had his arms in the air and broke them up and dispersed them.

'Gesu!' sighed Signora Nina.

Katerina Pariotis walked more quickly. The tanks were still there under the trees as were the accustomed blue, indifferent stares.

5

'General,' said Colonel Barge. 'The military situation on Cefalonia has become intolerable. Twice you have failed to accept our offers for your surrender. Now finally to safeguard the lives of my soldiers I am obliged to take certain necessary precautions.'

'I am just as concerned about the safety of your soldiers as I am about my own,' replied the general. 'In that case,' went on the colonel, 'it is even more urgent to reach a settlement. I cannot wait any longer.'

'I assure you, Colonel,' the general said, 'that I have no intention of putting the lives of your men in jeopardy, nor of my own. But after what has happened at Santa Maura, my officers and men have the right to be a little apprehensive.'

'If I understand you right,' answered the colonel, 'you do not trust the word of a German.' 'You understand correctly,' the general replied. 'Does it surprise you?' The colonel smiled. 'Yes,' he retorted, 'it does. Who signed the armistice with the Anglo-Americans? The Italians, not the Germans.' 'It was signed because the war is lost.' 'Lost by you, General.' 'It's lost,' repeated the general almost to himself, 'and to continue fighting is madness. It is madness for you, too.'

The colonel turned his head towards the window. The voices and the shouting reached them from the piazza and they heard the footsteps of the patrol and the cries of the soldiers.

'Your men are getting out of hand,' said the colonel. 'I hope that you will be able to keep them under control and that there will be no incidents. If my information is correct, there is a dangerous ill-feeling towards the German garrison.'

'My soldiers want to go home,' said the general. 'And we want to let them go home,' the colonel replied. 'We can reach a settlement that will allow them to go home.'

'We want to return to Italy with all our arms, not disarmed,' insisted the general.

The colonel did not understand him. 'What did you say?' he asked. 'The division will surrender Cefalonia to the Germans, if it is allowed to keep its armament intact,' repeated the general. 'Very well,' replied Colonel Barge. 'I will inform my government.' He said no more and left the room.

CHAPTER SIXTEEN

1

WHEN THE HORIZONS appeared unbounded why should escape be impossible?

The answer lay in the days and hours of indecision, the night at Lixourion, the uninterrupted flight of the Junkers, the betrayal of the army command, in the wireless signals, and the hesitation of the general. The cause of the sensation of being surrounded, of being in a trap about to be sprung unless someone prevented it, was coming at that very moment from the sea.

Three landing craft, loaded with arms and men, had appeared almost motionless in the evening light at the entrance to the bay. They looked like flotsam from some shipwreck drifting with a silent crew of corpses, but instead they carried picked troops and armoured vehicles to reinforce Colonel Barge's garrison. Aldo Puglisi could make them out clearly. He focussed his field glasses on them. He saw the soldiers' faces hidden by helmets coming down over their eyes. He saw the barrels of their rifles forming a bristling hedge of iron and behind the silent soldiers he saw the squat shapes of their vehicles.

In the evening light the three landing craft rose and fell with the scarcely perceptible movement of the sea. The boats would sink below the line of the horizon and then reappear suddenly closer in.

He thought that it was essential to spring the trap. The horizon was drawing nearer and was closing in on Cefalonia whilst up there on the hill behind Argostolion, with his new battery, he could raise a hand and stop the landing craft. It

120

was essential to keep the path to the horizon open, otherwise they would be deprived of the sky and of the air, and the division would find itself in the dark, suddenly plunged into the night.

He shouted the order to load and to get ready to fire on the three landing craft. His orders were unnecessary. His men were already at their stations staring at the sea in fascination. They had understood the necessity of stopping the boats and that it fell to them to do it that evening on the thirteenth day after so many evenings and sunsets of waiting.

Aldo Puglisi indicated the range and the target, and as he gave the order to fire on the German helmets, the clusters of metal barrels going up and down on the water and the wall of armoured vehicles, he felt himself in the grip of a wild exultation because it was he who was about to act against the orders of Supergreccia and the army command and to force the uncertain hand of the general. Without knowing what it was, he felt the pleasure of rediscovering the courage of his convictions and his own individuality after having been a part of a military machine, a cog in a hierarchy.

He gave the order to fire and as he did so he savoured the taste of rebellion and unaccustomed freedom, together with anxiety and the fear of the unknown.

Out from Argostolion the mirror of the sea burst open in white foam. The rhythm of the waves, until now so regular, became convulsed. The boats reared up towards the sky and then crashed down again disappearing in unexpected troughs in the sea only to leap high again. The silent crews who had been waiting like shadows massed together for the landing ran shouting from side to side of the boats.

As the captain heard the shots of his battery whose flashes added brilliance to the light of the setting sun, it seemed to him that their red hot barrels were firing in defence of some anonymous and indefinable someone who was standing beside him demanding revenge for suffering undergone. They were firing for the sad face of Katerina, for the peasant women dressed in black whom they had met along the route of their advance, for their own women, for Amalia, too, for the wives of his gunners whom other soldiers of other invading armies would meet in Italy on the route of their advance. They seemed to be firing against all uniforms and against Karl.

Then the guns stopped firing and the voices of German soldiers could be heard shouting for help.

The captain looked at the horizon free and open once more, cleared of arms and vehicles. Now the stretch of sea was settling down again, and returning to a normality that had been momentarily violated. The madness of savagery in the eyes of his men died away as they stood motionless beside their guns in the fading light.

'What will happen now?' he asked himself.

It was sunset and the guns of the battery smoked in the green shadows of the pinewood. He had only taken over command that afternoon. Only that morning he had been sleeping in Katerina's soft bed. And now, everything had been turned upside down, the rules of routine were broken, and Cefalonia was turned inside out like the lining of a glove.

But the horizon was there, intact. The paths to it were free again with all their possibilities. This was the only thing that mattered.

Two motor launches put out from the shore beneath Lixourion, the German flag fluttering in the breeze behind them. They made swiftly to where the heads were bobbing amongst pieces of wood and the last of the foam. A seaplane took off from behind the ridge and flew in the direction of Argostolion, and when it was in the middle of the gulf, as though it had given a signal, the tanks in the avenue by the eucalyptus opened fire. The noise ran along the trees, swept into the opening of Piazza Valianos, thundered through the streets of the town, re-echoing amongst the façades of the houses.

Aldo Puglisi and his gunners followed the first uncertain movements of the tanks. They left the shelter of the lane to advance nearer the piazza. The branches of eucalyptus which had been placed over the armour-plating fell from them like old clothes. Their guns blazed from their turrets at point blank range.

The captain turned to shout more orders to his gunners, but spontaneously they had gone back to their positions, training their guns on the advancing tanks. His order to fire was anticipated. Bursts of black earth rose amongst the tanks which turned rapidly and withdrew. They took up their original positions, in the shelter of the trees. The fire from their guns died down as though the Germans had not expected the reaction of the Italians and were stupefied by what was happening beyond the slits in their armour. Firing had broken out in the streets of the town too. Groups of infantry were running towards Piazza Valianos, to repulse the attack. The reports of rifle and machine gun fire and the dry rattle, like tin, of fire from light tanks were heard.

The seaplane had escaped notice. It had flown across the bay and passed high above the town. He saw tongues of fire and smoke burst out from a roof and the roof itself collapse as though some mysterious internal force had split it from top to bottom, leaving the interior of the house exposed in the dying light. On the same line of flight, in a perfect straight line, other roofs collapsed gently, opening up tiny coloured rooms to the skies toylike. Anti-aircraft guns opened fire from somewhere on the island and little black puffs exploded around the seaplane, but it avoided them easily and disappeared behind the ridges of the mountain.

The fire from the tanks by Piazza Valianos ceased. An armoured car with a white flag flying above its roof appeared on the bridge. Then the fire from the battery stopped and the shouting in the streets died down. Only the clouds of smoke remained hanging in mid air.

'Are the Germans surrendering?' Aldo Puglisi wondered incredulously. His gunners stood in their pits looking as he was at the flag that was fluttering towards Argostolion with the same question in their minds. They were wondering what was the significance of this white apparition waving above the grey roof of the armoured car. It travelled the length of the bridge, reflected in the dark water of the bay, and disappeared amongst the first houses of Argostolion, making its way towards the centre.

Were the Germans surrendering? Neither the captain nor his men could bring themselves to believe it. Nevertheless, after the gunfire they felt a strange sensation of calm. It seemed to them that after their gesture of defiance, they would be able to confront anything successfully and with impunity. For a moment they felt like soldiers, as they had never felt in the Albanian mountains or in the villages of Greece. They felt that even the Germans could be stopped, because they were made just like the Italians, cast in the same mould of flesh and blood. Together with their captain they had fired on their own initiative. Like him they had suffered the humiliation of the armistice, the exasperation of waiting, the sense of betrayal, and now it was as if all that had never been.

At any minute down there the German envoys would be getting out of their armoured car in Piazza Valianos. A few rounds of gunfire, the landing craft sent to the bottom, a check to the panzers, had been enough to make Colonel Barge realize what the situation was. 'Could it be possible?' Aldo Puglisi wondered.

The soldiers looked down at the town with their eyes screwed up against the dazzle of the setting sun, wry smiles on their lips, uncertain whether to believe their eyes or not, to shout out, to jump on the limbers, to dance on the shells, or throw their helmets in the air. They felt they had reached the outer edge of resistance, but at the same time they were afraid that they were wrong. They sat amongst their guns and the shells piled on the ground. They looked at the town and at the sea, smoking cigarettes which they concealed in their hands black with oil and smoke. They spoke quietly with a kind of shame.

The sun dropped below the horizon. The clouds of smoke from the roofless houses disappeared into the sky. Out in the bay the German motor launches had finished picking up the survivors and they made towards the west beach at Lixourion. A squadron of Junkers transport planes appeared overhead, flying in perfect arrowhead formation. They caught the rays of the vanished sun, and lit up against the shadows of twilight they looked like great monstrous mechanical birds painted pink.

The soldiers looked up at them. The little black crosses stood out on the fuselages more and more plainly, and when they were clearly visible the birds of steel were transformed into a procession of flying coffins. These dark crosses on the sides and wings of the planes seemed to give the captain and his men, as they looked upwards, confirmation of their disbelief and to destroy their hopes.

'They are still receiving reinforcements, sir,' a voice said, and it had a tone of sadness. Already the enthusiasm of victory, childish though it had been, was gone.

The field telephone rang to summon Captain Puglisi to headquarters. 'Have the Germans surrendered?' he asked into the mouthpiece. But he was answered with an oath. 'What do you mean?' the operator said, 'Surrendered? No. It's a truce; they've asked for a truce.' Aldo Puglisi hung up the receiver. He felt weary.

Officers and men stood crowding round him. 'Have they surrendered?' was their silent question, and without speaking he answered 'No'. He sat down on the nearest ammunition box and passed his hand over his face. It grated on his stubby chin. He had not shaved for several days. His shirt and his vest were dirty too. His body smelt of sweat, and oil, of petrol and hot metal. He smelt of war. He told Gerace to get some water, soap and a nail brush, a clean shirt and a change of underwear, just as if he was going off to an assignation.

'Going out with your girl friend?' said Gerace, trying to joke, but his eyes were dull and he spoke without animation.

When he got up from the box, he saw the armoured car reappear on the bridge. It came from the road to Argostolion, without its white flag, and was lost in the first shadows of night. The two motor launches had disappeared. A great silence fell over the sea and the mountains, the plain and the scarred city. It fell round the guns and the artillerymen. He listened to it whilst he shaved. He rubbed lotion into his dried up skin and looked at himself carefully in the mirror.

He was still himself on Cefalonia, with a past behind him, a wife and a son who were waiting for him at home, and Katerina in her little house on the road to San Teodoro. It was he, an officer in an organized army, who had broken its code of discipline by giving his own unauthorized order to open fire on the Germans, and had made a gesture against authority.

He looked at himself attentively to see if without knowing it or wanting it he was some sort of hero. But no, he was no hero. He had just obeyed the orders of the legitimate government. That would be a good defence tomorrow in front of the court martial. Then, even though the exaltation was past, he felt calmer.

2

From the hill at Lixourion, Karl Ritter had followed what had been happening. He stood near the telephone waiting patiently for the operator in the mechanical citadel, the city of iron and fire which was behind him, all round him and in front of him, to tell him what to do.

But no order to attack reached him; only to wait, unmoving at his post.

He had obeyed while he watched the sequence of events; the sinking of the landing craft, the seaplane and the tanks opening fire. He followed it all attentively and could not manage to make it out at all. He could not make himself understand how the Italians could have sunk so low into the ignominy of this treachery.

Above all he could not understand why they did not realize that they were digging their own graves.

CHAPTER SEVENTEEN

1

THEN NIGHT HAD fallen in all its intensity. A truce had been signed with the Germans and the officers' conference was over.

There was no sound of machine guns or mortars, nor the engines of Junkers, not even of the clatter of steel tracks on the roads and fields. Cefalonia was sleeping the calm sleep of a Mediterranean night.

He had stopped by the Pariotises' garden with the intention of calling on Katerina and of sitting beside her in the garden, and talking. But now the inclination left him. The shutters of her room were closed and between the slats he saw a faint orange light which must have come from the lamp beneath the picture of the saint. There was no sound of footsteps or voices.

What would they have talked about? That evening he could not have managed to bear the face so like the face of Amalia but darker and more sorrowful. He could not have got out one word of all that was going on within him. He would have apologized to her and, as had already happened, she would have continued not to understand him, and she would have gone on looking at him, her eyes getting bigger and bigger and more moist, forgiving him.

It was not for pity that he felt the need, but rather for contempt and hate. For this reason he left the garden behind him and went away with the feeling of walking on tiptoe as though leaving a world where he did not belong, into which he had forced an entry. He retraced the road into the town. He met the curfew patrol of carabinieri and cavalry. The hooves of horses resounded sharply amongst the houses, like pieces of metal hammered in the night. In Piazza Valianos, he stopped to look around. There was something senseless in the coming and going of the patrol across the piazza. Feeling the need for a drink he went towards Nicolino's café, but its glass door was barred and the space reserved for tables was empty. Little Nicolino was asleep behind the closed windows of the upper floor, or perhaps he was peering out at the movements of the patrol.

He looked around at Piazza Valianos with its clump of palm trees pointing to a sky dripping with stars, the wrought-iron lamps, the familiar façade of the headquarters and this pavement where so often they had sat drinking and gossiping amongst themselves, or with Signora Nina's girls, watching the people go by and listening to the divisional band concerts. All these had become familiar during months of garrison duty. The faces in the café, the jokes, the billiards, laughter suddenly vanishing into the emptiness of the night, and then the drive along by the sea, the sea mills, and Katerina's little room with the old chest of drawers and the faded mirror. Slowly, day by day, without his really noticing it, all this had become part of his life.

Only now when he was on the point of leaving it for ever did he realize it. He wondered if once he was back in Italy again he would think of Cefalonia with nostalgia as he did now of home.

At the idea of returning to Italy, he smiled sadly. There was the sea to be reckoned with and Colonel Barge's soldiers who, although since the encounter at dusk had been as if paralyzed in their positions, were on their guard. He felt the lenses of Colonel Barge's field glasses trained on him, and the cold blue eyes of Karl staring indifferently at him from the hill above Lixourion where he and his guns were concealed.

Still walking he started out again along the road to his battery. Beneath the gaze of the field glasses and the cold blue eyes his footsteps became uneasy.

He stopped near a little wooden bridge and looking slowly round him lit a cigarette. He tried to make out the slopes of

Lixourion, but the mountain was wrapped in darkness and there was no sign of a gun nor even a light. Beneath his feet a little stream murmured on its way down to the shore. He leant on the rails of the bridge and watched the sparkling water as it hurried to lose itself in the sea. From where he was every trace of the landing craft had vanished and the sea looked calm and clean. He imagined German soldiers in combat dress slowly sinking beneath the unbroken surface of the sea, their machine pistols at the ready, arms and legs open like rubber dolls drawn down towards the valleys and peaks of subterranean mountains.

It was he with his coastal guns who had sent them down there. These dolls with their clumsy movements were his work. Instead of feeling satisfied he had a sensation of distress, of physical revulsion as though he had bitten into something tainted. It was the first time since he had put on a uniform that he knew for sure that he had killed someone. A sort of anguish forced him away from the bridge and he started walking again to prevent himself from being overcome by it. He was not made of the stuff of heroes or warriors, he knew it, nor even of a battery commander. As the hours, days and nights passed and more new circumstances arose, the better he understood it. He was born for a modest, colourless civilian life, to be passed between the grey walls of his home town, an inglorious life as a civil engineer.

2

'Gentlemen, it was a grave mistake to attack the German landing craft.'

'Gentlemen, are the troops under your command prepared to fight?'

The questions that the general had asked at the officers' conference echoed senselessly in his ears. He would never succeed, never, in overcoming his disgust for those drowned puppets. Nor would his gunners, who had been born to cultivate their vines and fields. Certainly, at that moment they, too, were looking at that space of unbroken sea, thinking with distaste of the flaccid corpses of their victims sinking down.

They had crowded silently into the narrow corridors, dark hallways and smoke filled rooms of headquarters, surprised to find everybody there at the same meeting, even the junior officers. Were they all to be tried by court martial, Aldo Puglisi wondered.

'You realize that by taking the initiative we could overcome the Germans,' the general said and his voice was remote like the voice of another person.

Aldo Puglisi tried to examine the features of his face, but in the half light from the petrol lamp they could not be seen clearly, remaining confused and indistinct. Instead he was able to see his hands. They were motionless, almost transparent, so white were they in the pool of light from the lamp which fell on the surface of the table. It was a circle of violet light completely detached from the surrounding shadow. Within it the hands appeared as though they were made of wax.

The officers had replied to the general's question in the affirmative. The silence turned to a babble of voices and sound which spread rapidly from office to office, from corridor to corridor to the hallway and courtyard of headquarters. The general half raised his hands in the light of the lamp as though such a response surprised him. They remained poised as if listening and then returned with hesitation to their place on the table.

'Don't be under any illusions. The German Air Force would destroy us,' he said, though it seemed that it was his hands that spoke.

At the chorus of voices and the protests of the officers, the hands had stiffened. They had turned on their backs to show their empty palms. Then, with clenched fists they had left the circle of light to climb up to the general's brow which was lost in the shadows from the lamp. Without listening to the voices of his colleagues, but thinking mechanically that at last someone had asked them their opinion, Aldo Puglisi watched the hands fascinated as though they were two acrobats performing in the circus ring.

The hands had reappeared in the circle of light. They were clasped nervously together and then relaxed while the distant voice of the general expounded the risks to which the division would expose itself by not accepting an honourable settlement. The division did not have one fighter aircraft to support it, nor could it count on help from Italy or Supergreccia. They could count solely on their own resources, which were at that moment, it was true, superior to the German forces, but would be inferior taking into account the inevitable intervention of the German Air Force.

'Santa Maura, Santa Maura!' the officers cried. The hands of the general had raised themselves up within the circle of light and motionless in the air had commanded silence.

The division would never leave Cefalonia without its arms, they had said. The division would leave the island to the Germans without a fight only if Colonel Barge would agree that they kept possession of all their weapons. Such an agreement, the hands had concluded, would have to carry the signature of Hitler as a guarantee.

There was silence. The general's last words were finished without an echo in the heavy silence of the headquarters. Aldo Puglisi had sought out his eyes in the veil of shadow. He imagined that if he had succeeded in meeting them they would have been reflecting the same thoughts, the same fears and even the same pale image of the colonel as did his own.

'Explain the situation to your men,' the general had concluded. After a moment of uncertainty, as though he were on the point of saying something more, he had got up wearily, as if the whole weight of the division bore down upon his shoulders. His hands travelled up through the light and disappeared into the shadows. He came towards the officers who drew apart to let him pass.

Aldo Puglisi saw the outline of his gun emplacements. Up there in a little while he would have to explain the situation to his men who were waiting to hear about his court martial. But what would he be able to tell them? They would have answered him that it was too late to ask their opinion now;

the general and the captain, too, ought to have asked them years before when they had first enlisted and dressed up as soldiers. He himself bore his part of the responsibility. He had helped to dress them in soldiers' uniform. He was guilty, not only towards Katerina Pariotis, Nicolino, and the Greek people, but towards his own men and towards himself. And perhaps, too, he thought, in some way even his men were guilty in allowing themselves to be dressed up.

He stopped in surprise, surprised at having discovered only then, this simple, elementary truth.

3

The officers questioned their men who replied that they would rather fight the Germans than lay down their arms and be taken prisoners. Thus the general had official confirmation of a feeling of which he was already aware and which had already found expression in other ways; the killing of the captain who had extolled the alliance with the Germans; the flag torn from the wing of his car and the sinking of the landing craft.

Captain Puglisi's men expressed their determination to fight; Gerace, too; and the captain said to himself, 'Listen to them, they're heroes!' But he knew quite well that not one of them, himself included, was anything like a hero. He saw the shadow of Santa Maura across their faces. He felt that there was only one thing that was still important: to forestall the Germans, get home, and once and for all put an end to this ridiculous war.

4

On the fourteenth day an understanding between the Italian and German commands had been reached. In spite of the reported feelings of his soldiers, the Italian general had tried once more to find a way out which would safeguard the honour of the division and at the same time be acceptable to the Germans.

'No laying down of arms and repatriation of the division with Hitler's signature as a guarantee,' he had proposed. Colonel Barge had agreed. Since the sinking of the landing craft in the bay and the engagement on the Argostolion road, it had been borne in upon him that the Italian soldiers were more disposed to fight than he could reasonably have expected. Therefore he had said that he would agree to the general's demands and had also promised that the harbour of Argostolion should remain under the Italian flag and that he would have the flights of the Junkers stopped.

In each of the opposing groups there was surprise mixed with distrust. Oberleutnant Ritter tried to find his own explanation for the unexpected turn of events and then gave up the attempt. If the colonel had arranged things like this, then it must be all right. Captain Puglisi tried to hope, without much conviction, that the promises would be kept. He looked around him and could still see no sign of Italian ships, either in the harbour or on the horizon, and he wondered how and when the division could embark with all its arms both light and heavy. He felt, and with him all his gunners, and with them the rest of the division, that there was something unlikely and unreal in what was going on. They had the feeling that it was all too simple and easy and that Colonel Barge was laying a trap for them.

Next day at ten o'clock in the fresh light of morning the wings of the Junker had appeared against the blue sky. Then in full, slow, humming circles, it had come lower. The hum had grown into a roar and finally it landed delicately on the surface of the water.

Its flight was followed by the anxious eyes of the Italians and more casually by the Germans. Such of the inhabitants of Argostolion and Lixourion who knew of the surrender terms watched it too, wondering what would happen now. Amongst these was Katerina Pariotis. Beyond the flowers in

133

her garden, her dark eyes, filled with alarm, saw that the plane was real and not a bad dream. It had furrowed a path across the sea and was moored in the usual place.

Signora Nina heard it more clearly than the other people in the town. It had nearly taken off the roof of the villa. She had run to the window calling the girls. They had all hung out to look with their eyes wide open and then shut them against the brilliant light. Their hair was in disorder and their faces were unpainted and swollen with sleep. 'What is it, what's happening?' La Triestina who could only see white shadows in front of her had asked. 'Oh,' moaned Adriana, 'why can't the bloody fools leave us in peace.' Signora Nina crossed herself as the plane was moored. 'Gesu,' she said. 'Let me go, girls. Let me go and see the skipper of the caique.' But not one of the girls was trying to stop her.

Pasquale Lacerba, the photographer, had watched the plane too, from the window of his office, seated behind his desk where he was translating an Italian proclamation into Greek. It ordered the Cefaliots to keep calm, to observe the curfew, and not to hinder the administration of the island in any way. Pasquale Lacerba grew pale as he watched the mooring of the seaplane. He remained tense and silent for what seemed hours, even years seated at the old worn desk from the post office which the Italians had given him. He waited for it.

And then at last when he heard the first gunfire from the anti-aircraft battery, he relaxed and felt almost happy as though freed from some danger. He knew for certain now that the war had started between the Italians and Germans.

5

The flight of Stukas did not appear in the sky at Cefalonia until about 2.30 in the afternoon, a little late according to Oberleutnant Ritter's expectations, but it arrived and without hesitation dived in formation at the Italian positions on the coast, as though the pilots already knew the exact location of the batteries, almost as though they had flown this mission before. With his face to the sun as it beat down from the blazing sky of early afternoon, he watched their flight. He felt happy. His confidence and strength returned.

And now the show began. Karl Ritter forgot the Italians and Cefalonia. As always, the perfect manoeuvres of the Stukas and their furious attacks succeeded in transforming him from a soldier into just an admiring spectator. They hung up there, with their swept back wings, almost motionless in the air, and then he saw them slowly roll over to one side and slip towards the earth, cutting a perpendicular line through space, hurtling on to their objectives.

Each time the moment of suspense between life and death was repeated, it seemed that at this point the pilots, as though bewitched, were abandoning themselves to self destruction.

Even now, after years of war, Oberleutnant Ritter had to struggle to hide his emotion at this spectacle from his men. He had to force himself to keep his eyes fixed on the spot upon which the aeroplanes were diving, preceded by the mechanical scream of the sirens which they carried. They skimmed over the enemy batteries, the coast road and the rocks on the shore. Then regaining height they wove their way safely through the intricate network of trees, and climbed again up into the sky leaving behind them smoke, flame and noise.

The Italian batteries across the bay on the Argostolion peninsula were being blown into the air.

From where he was above Lixourion he could make out through his field-glasses the gun emplacements as they reappeared, battered and broken, from behind the curtain of dust and smoke as the sea breeze cleared it away. He could see the gun crews running through the surrounding trees, swarming round the limbers and carrying the ammunition to safety.

Ready at his post with his platoon at the alert around him, Karl Ritter scented in the air the exciting smell of fire, splintered rock, torn earth, the smell of war compounded from burning petrol, synthetic rubber, overheated metal, and engine oil.

As though they were playing some game the Stukas made off towards the horizon, in a disordered dance. They re-appeared to the east of the island and once more seemed to make straight for their objectives without having to seek them out. They dived to the level of the roofs of Argostolion and plunged down towards the white of the road to Capo San Teodoro, beyond the sports ground and the eucalyptus avenue on the outskirts of the town. The oberleutnant lowered his glasses and on the other side of the bay on the San Teodoro road he saw a column of vehicles. He saw it stop and writhe like a wounded snake. Italian infantry, hindered by their ridiculous uniforms, jumped out of the vehicles and sought cover amongst the rocks on the shore or in the gardens of the Greek houses. In a few moments the road disappeared in a cloud of smoke.

To protect the German garrison scattered through the hills, which would have been easy prey for the superior Italian forces, the colonel was concentrating his attack on the Argosto-lion peninsula. It was there that the greater part of the Italian division was deployed. Right from the start it was necessary to hit the enemy at his strongest point, to prevent all possibility of retaliation. It was essential to strike the enemy hard, right to the heart, and the enemy's heart beat round the yellow roofs of Argostolion, around the towers of Aghios Spiridion, Aghios Nicolaos, Aghios Gerasimos and the ten orthodox saints. The heart of the enemy beat, too, on the hill at the back of the town, and further away on the other side of the island, invisible from Lixourion. It was necessary to destroy the division before it put its nose outside its den, before it could move its men and its vehicles along the few available roads. It must be done before sunset when the activities of the Stukas would have to stop. It had to happen quickly.

It was what Aldo Puglisi was saying, too. It had to happen quickly. Something had to be done quickly to escape death. From his post in the tower of Aghios Nicolaos' church, he saw before him the whole of Cefalonia almost complete within its framework of roofs and roads, hills and sea, plains and woods. It puzzled him that so small an island could contain a war. The idea occurred to him that probably, like an old gunboat motionless at anchor without means of defence, the island would sink to the bottom of the sea if the Stukas continued their bombardment much longer.

'The Stukas,' Aldo Puglisi had shouted in blind, senseless rage, as he had seen them approaching, and Gerace, who was climbing up behind him, had halted on the wooden stairs and ducked his head between his shoulders, more like a child than a man, a child with a black beard, days old. He shut his eyes as Aldo Puglisi did, too, until the wave of sound had disappeared into the distance.

Yes, he had told himself, as he drew himself up again to the narrow window, like a loophole in an old fortress, the general had been right and now all of them and Cefalonia too would be lost in the waters of the Mediterranean. Or, he wondered again, had the general been wrong, wrong in wasting so much time in negotiations, in trying to reach an agreement and allowing the Germans to get reinforcements?

The captain picked out the sports ground behind the double row of eucalyptus trees. On its rectangle of grass the German troop carriers were drawn up. From the tower of Aghios Nicolaos he had to direct the fire of the artillery into this small area. The fire control lacked a suitable observation post and so he had been sent up the highest tower in the city. Aldo Puglisi wrote the necessary instructions on a page of a signal pad and handed it to Gerace who ran down the stairs almost falling into the street where a dispatch rider was waiting on a motorcycle, its engine running. He sped off, skidding on the curve, but recovered balance on the road to Piazza Valianos, and disappeared silently, the noise of the motorcycle lost in the greater sound of war.

Amalia, Katerina Pariotis, his son; Aldo Puglisi thought of them all without being able to feel either emotion or interest. At this moment their names meant absolutely nothing to him. He could scarcely recall their faces in the smoke of the bombardment which seemed to blot out even memory. Nothing, he was forced to realize, was going to arouse his interest or emotion, not even the artillery fire which was beginning to fall nearer the sports ground, nearer and nearer, and which would soon, thanks to the information he had sent down, be on the target; not even the small arms fire that had opened up on them from down below.

'Captain, they have spotted us,' Gerace shouted from the stairs.

They were shooting at him, the captain in the tower. He flattened himself with his back to a corner. Something struck the bell, perhaps it was he himself who had hit it in his hurry to take cover. The bell tolled and its reverberation echoed to and fro in the dark well of the tower, confused with the shots of machine guns and rifles.

Then the firing died down, but the scream of the Stukas' sirens and the roar of the artillery remained. Aldo Puglisi looked through the slit at Cefalonia and tried to make out the roof of Katerina's house. He could see Lixourion plainly on the other side of the bay. He wondered if Karl Ritter was still there. And Signora Nina with her peroxided and painted girls – where were they at this moment, and were they frightened or amused? And old Matias and his dilapidated carriage, what part of the island had he got to?

Machine gunfire opened up again and Aldo Puglisi had to drop to his knees on the brick floor. It seemed to be coming from the technical school. It was plain that the Germans had spotted him and were firing at him from the roof or windows of the building. They were shooting at him as though he was a bird.

'Let's get out of here,' shouted Gerace retreating down the stairs.

The bell tower shook like a flag in the wind. The bell was hit. There was a dry sound of the bullet ricocheting and the bronze gave out a soft moan. Gerace snatched his hand from the rail of the stairs. It was wet with blood. 'Captain, I am hit,' he said in astonishment.

But the captain took no notice. An unnatural calm had taken possession of him. He knew with mathematical certainty that if he wanted to cheat death he had to wait until the shooting from the technical school stopped and go on transmitting fire orders. Between him and death a sort of competition started, between death and the whole division.

'Captain,' repeated Gerace, as he sat on the ladder looking at his hand red with blood, 'Captain.' He spoke more by way of lament than of expecting an answer.

Aldo Puglisi was not listening to him. He was looking out of the narrow window, following the flight of the Stukas as they pulled out again towards the sky. He saw the profile of a face in a cockpit. It was the fourth or fifth time, he had lost count, that they had dived down and zoomed away again.

'They'll blow us to bits, if it doesn't get dark soon,' he thought, looking at the sun. If only night would fall then the Stukas would be called off and things might take a turn for the better.

The sun set at about seven in the evening and the Stukas made off across the sea and did not return. Then detachments of Italian infantry came out into the streets and on to the slopes of the hills and the isolated German units on the Argostolion peninsula had to withdraw to higher ground towards Col del Telegrafo.

Up there, deployed amongst the pines, they opened fire with their automatic weapons. The long, coloured trails of tracer bullets lit up the night. Captain Aldo Puglisi and the gunners in their pits were reminded of fireworks at a country festa.

Oberleutnant Ritter saw it all, too, but to him it was just war. He led his platoon swiftly down to the landing place. The moon was rising from behind the mass of Enos. It was clear and transparent like a paper stage prop. It threw the flank of the distant mountain and its valleys into relief, but the lighters anchored by the shore remained in the shadows as did the waters of the bay. The moonlight would not reach them for some hours.

He looked at the boats. They were close in to Lixourion. He noticed that they were not proper landing craft, but primitive barges improvised by the engineers from tables nailed together like rafts from a shipwreck. The flotilla rocked gently between the rocks and the gurgling sea wells, swaying beneath the feet of its cargo of soldiers. They put out from the shore, weighed down with their burden. Slowly and silently they gained the open water, their bows pointing towards the centre of the bay. The black wall of the mountain, with Col del Telegrafo lit up in the background, rocked before Karl Ritter's eyes as they searched the darkness. First it tipped to the right and then to the left. Then it seemed to regain its balance and come towards the lights faster and faster.

Karl Ritter tightened his grip on the butt of his machine pistol as the wall came closer. The moment he had been waiting for the whole afternoon had come. He savoured the last slow passing minutes before battle. It was just a battle, he thought, scanning the opposite shore, a battle of revenge. From a totally unexpected quarter he was going to throw himself on the enemy's rear. Like the sharp blade of a knife he was going to cut across the hill behind Col del Telegrafo and take the Italian infantry by surprise. He would have annihilated them before the moon would be halfway across the sky. He had plenty of time. He had worked out the different stages of the action as though for a sports meeting.

His heart gave a jump and he brought his hands up to his eyes. Two dazzling, cold white beams of light suddenly illuminated the glass-like sea, laying bare stretches of transparent, gently undulating water, moving corridors of light probing into the depths of the night. The two searchlights were coming from the shore at San Teodoro. They moved like a fan sweeping the surface of the water in opposite directions, searching out the two shores and the sea.

Karl Ritter's thoughts became confused. Without succeeding in formulating words or exact images, he realized instinctively that it was something to do with the searchlight unit of the Italian Navy which had been moved from Argostolion to some point on the coast and that they, the Germans, had allowed themselves to be caught in a trap. Rage mixed with a feeling of impotence almost choked him, out there in the middle of the sea. It was not fear of the empty expanse around him revealed by the Italian searchlights. It was the rage of impotence.

Silently the two tones of light surrounded the invasion fleet. The rafts, the motor boats, each man's face and weapons, were picked out by the dazzling beam. There was a long drawn out moment of expectation and then the naval batteries above Argostolion opened fire, and the moment of waiting was over. The unbroken surface of the bay came to life. The leading boat sank and Karl Ritter threw himself into the water.

In the motionless beam of the searchlights, he felt the silence descend again. He looked round him and there in the midst of the wreckage of the lighter he saw the bodies of his men bobbing up and down like so much flotsam. The Italians were not firing any more. From the coast road someone shouted out something to them. Italian soldiers jumped into the sea and started swimming out towards them. A motor boat put out from the shore and came towards the wreckage. The Italian soldiers shouted encouragingly and stretched out their hands to drag the survivors on board. But Karl Ritter made no move. He remained lying on his pneumatic raft, his head on one side, bobbing up and down amongst his dead soldiers, until the voices of the Italians were silent and the motor boat had turned its bow towards Argostolion with its load of prisoners. Karl Ritter calculated that there were about thirty prisoners out of the three hundred and fifty who had embarked.

The searchlights went out and the darkness closed in. Even Col del Telegrafo was now without light. The hail of tracer had ceased and Karl Ritter thought that even his comrades up there had been wiped out or captured.

He slipped into the water and cautiously pushed his raft in front of him. So dazzling had the naval searchlights been that the darkness now seemed very dense and he could hardly see the coast at Lixourion. A whitish clump of bushes was just visible on the mountain and he set his course by it. The raft would help to hide him when the moon rose higher over the tops of the hills.

It was not exactly a presentiment of death that he felt on the morning of the 17th, but he sensed that disaster was not far off. The German reconnaissance plane reached the island in the first light of a pale, reluctant dawn. It flew along the hills, over the gulf and turned up the valley. Aldo Puglisi knew that it was looking for something in the shadows that were hanging between the fading night and the still unborn day.

It dropped three flares which burst with a vivid red flame against the background of the hills. From the bridge at Argostolion to the old fortress at San Giorgio everything became plainly visible. Then the plane flew off out to sea leaving its flares swaying as though suspended by invisible wires. With tantalizing slowness, they sank irresistibly towards the ground. The shadows of the mountains, houses and trees lengthened. Amongst the shadows were the infantry and the horses of the 1st Battalion, 317th Regiment, in full battle order, waiting on the road for the signal to move against the German positions.

7

Then there was silence again and it seemed to be going to last. It was not just an interval between one flight of twin-engined bombers and the next. The waves of roaring metallic sound that had ploughed up the earth seemed definitely to have stopped.

Yes, the silence was real and lasting, strange after the uproar of bombs and anti-aircraft guns. Katerina looked around her at the walls of the room. The picture of Aghios Nicolaos, the photograph of the captain on the chest of drawers, the hanging lamp in the living-room. Everything had now recovered its natural equilibrium and was in its usual place as if life had never known violence.

Katerina Pariotis went out into the garden. The flower beds were still there with all their blooms, the steps in the path leading down to the road were intact and the road itself stretched straight, the purest white in the midday sun. There were still the sea mills, undamaged down by the shore, and the lighthouse still rose up out of the water although the seagulls had gone.

But when she turned towards the town she saw what she expected. A cloud of smoke rose above the tops of the pine trees forming a great billowing umbrella which was spreading ponderously up towards the English cemetery and over to the other side of the island. Other drifts of blue smoke rose up from the fields, the olive groves, the plain, and from the roads where the dive bombers had come down low to machine gun the anti-aircraft positions and the Italian soldiers.

Katerina Pariotis thought distractedly of Aldo Puglisi. The German machine guns would have been searching for him, too. Perhaps he was dead.

She went down the road walking towards the town. Her pace became faster and faster until she was almost running. As she got closer to it, the burning town drew her more and more urgently. She ran drawn by the flames and the growing clamour of voices. Down paths from the hills other women were pouring into the road, alone or holding children by the hand, and old men, too. They reached the road in search of safety. They were escaping from their bombed or machine-gunned villages to gaze upon an even greater disaster and to feel the presence of their fellow men around them.

Katerina Pariotis paused for breath. In the eucalyptus avenue the German tanks had withdrawn and a column of Italian troop carriers and infantry with their rifles slung, their packs on their backs, were advancing in silence.

A motorcyclist cleared a way through the crowd for the troop carriers. They were heading towards Capo San Teodoro. The grim, exhausted faces of the soldiers looked down from the troop carriers. Someone in the crowd greeted them and waved his hand. Some of the soldiers answered but they were already in the distance. The soldiers on foot who were following shouted that the people should not go into the town and that the civilians should keep well away from Argostolion. But the crowd of fugitives continued to struggle forward towards the town, taking no notice of the warning.

'Bella bambina,' a soldier shouted. Other voices joined in down the double file of rifles. There was a burst of laughter and the sharp sound of the points of fingers being kissed. Katerina Pariotis smiled at them, searching the faces of the officers who marched at the side of the column.

'Captain Puglisi, the artillery captain Aldo Puglisi, does anyone know him?' she would have liked to have asked. 'Can anyone tell me where he is? Is he dead?'

The column passed and the voices and the footsteps were lost in the direction of the sea. She found herself once more in the middle of the crowd in Piazza Valianos looking at a town stripped naked with its entrails exposed.

The houses which were still standing were roofless with their outer walls missing. Rooms were left hanging in the air, yellow, red and blue, with tables and beds still in place, a picture on the wall, electric lights hanging from the ceiling, a vase of flowers on the windowsill.

Men and women were hurrying through the streets. They were loading carts with their household goods. They drew them by hand, the men between the shafts, the women, the old people and their children pushing behind. They were making towards Kuvatos in the open country, or towards the bridge away from the smoke and rubble, away from the noise of sirens and aeroplane engines. Amidst the shouting and the weeping an acrid smell of rubble hung in the air.

Katerina's gaze fell on the building of the elementary school. Its front wall lay in ruins across the street. The passage on the upper floor was gone, leaving the doorways of the classrooms open, with their dark wood desks lined up in front of the teacher's dais, and the blackboards and the maps still hanging on the walls.

She hurried on across the piazza and found herself once more in the thick of the crowd where company seemed to make the disaster less fearful. But when she reached the headquarters building, she left the stream of people and halted, weary and dispirited. She sat on the wall and watched the officers as they went up and down the steps, came and went in their cars. All the Italian officers were there. She recognized the familiar faces which she had seen countless times at the military band concerts and in the cafés round the piazza. They all seemed to be there except Aldo Puglisi and the fear that he was dead returned again and became a certainty. The tears that she had been choking back for so long came to her eyes. She wept in silence, for an ex-enemy captain, whom at one time she had hated, and who was now dead, somewhere in the island.

'He is dead,' thought Katerina, putting a hand over her eyes to hide her tears.

She dried her eyes. Now that she had given way to her feelings she felt better and able to continue her search. After all, she had only given way to her fears. The captain could perfectly well be safe like the officers and soldiers moving around her. They were everywhere, walking among the ruins, helping to move the carts, to rescue the injured, carrying them to Red Cross ambulances. He could very well be alive.

She got up and timidly immersed herself again in the turmoil of soldiers and vehicles. She turned once more towards Piazza Valianos. It seemed as though it was not she herself but another who was walking, looking and thinking in her place. She let herself go on, carried along by the flow of the crowd. She felt that its movement was not random, and that it had some secret purpose behind it. It might perhaps take her to the living Captain Aldo Puglisi.

He came from the piazza towards the headquarters as though he had been waiting for her all that time. He took her hands between his and showing no surprise at seeing her drew her gently away from the crowd. She too felt no surprise although a few minutes before she had believed that he was dead.

'Kyria,' the captain said, looking at her. His eyes had an unaccustomed light in them. His face had become thinner in the last few days and was unshaved and dark.

'Kyria,' he repeated and looked both happy and worried. 'What are you doing here?' he reproved her. 'Go back home, Kyria, go home quickly.'

'I am here because I love you,' thought Katerina. But she could not make herself say it. Her lips were hardly moving. And now, tears came again to her eyes.

His dry firm hand touched her hair, her cheeks and her lips in a long caress, whilst behind him the crowd flowed on, indistinct and confused, dragging carts loaded with bundles, baskets and trunks.

'Piccola Kyria,' said the captain.

Even though she had not actually said it, had he understood just the same? She hoped so. With all her strength she wanted it so to be. She thanked God for having made her meet him. At last, she thought, now the captain knew. And even if he had to die, he knew that he was not quite alone in a foreign land.

He took her back across the piazza to the eucalyptus avenue. 'We must hurry,' he said. 'The aeroplanes will come back any minute. I am going to take you home.'

But even if they had come back at that moment, she would not have fled. She felt safe and happy now. She would not have minded dying beside him, arm in arm with him, as they walked along.

CHAPTER EIGHTEEN

1

'ITALIANS OF CEFALONIA! Comrades! Italians, officers and men!

'Why are you fighting against the Germans? You have been betrayed by your leaders! Do you want to return to your country to be with your womenfolk, your children and your families? Well, the shortest way to get back to your country is certainly not by way of a British internment camp. You know already of the infamous conditions imposed on your country under the Anglo-American armistice.

'After they have made you betray your German brothers-in-arms, they will humiliate you with forced labour in the mines of Britain and Australia where manpower is short. Your leaders want to sell you to the British. Do not trust them.

'Follow the example of your comrades cut off in Greece, on Rhodes and on the other islands, who have all laid down their arms and have already been repatriated. In Rome and in other places in your homeland they have laid down their arms too.

'Yet you, now that a return to your homeland lies within your grasp, you prefer death and slavery under the British. We beseech you, do not force the German Stukas to sow death and destruction amongst you.

'Lay down your arms! The path home will be opened to you by your German comrades.

'With the betrayal by Badoglio, Fascist Italy and National Socialist Germany have been abandoned in their fateful struggle.

'The Italian Army in Greece has already finished laying down its arms without bloodshed. Only the Acqui Division, cut off on the islands of Cefalonia and Corfu, and completely isolated, commanded by General Gandin, a follower of Badoglio, has rejected the offer of a peaceful surrender and has turned on its German and Fascist comrades.

'This battle is absolutely without hope of victory for you. Your division, split in two, is surrounded by the sea. You have no reinforcements and are without the possibility of help from our enemies.

'We your German comrades do not want this battle. We beg you therefore to lay down your arms and to entrust yourselves to the German garrison on the island.

'The path home is open to you too, as it is to your other Italian comrades.

'If however you continue your present senseless resistance, within a few days you will be crushed and wiped out by the superior German forces which are being assembled. Anyone who is then taken prisoner will no longer be able to return home.

'Therefore, Italian comrades, as soon as this leaflet reaches you, make your way to the German lines.

'It is your last chance of safety!'

THE GERMAN GENERAL COMMANDING THE
ARMY CORPS.

The leaflets showered down on the Italian positions. It was a strange, fluttering, rustling rain of paper, falling diagonally after the aeroplane had flown off into the distance. Part of it, caught in the slipstream from the engines, proceeded on its own course horizontal to the ground. It moved across the bay like a flock of birds and came down out to sea where no one would find it.

Aldo Puglisi was reminded of the little single-engined plane looking as if it were made of tin which used to fly above the crowded beach on summer mornings when he was a boy. The pilot, his head plainly visible in a leather helmet, used to lean out of the open cockpit to shower handfuls of advertisements down on to the holidaymakers. They too used to come floating down following the wind. Many of them finished up far out to sea, others came down in the middle of the white beach rafts and sailing boats and on the landing stage. The boys used to chase them shouting along the edge of the sea, trying to catch them in the air.

He reread the leaflet. His gunners read them too. There were smiles on their unshaven faces and they joked to hide their fear. Since they had started to fire their guns, they had nothing about them of the peasant. They seemed to be a cross between motor mechanics and primitive warriors, warriors who had fought with stones and spears, not with guns. While they were pretending to be amused by the German threats, they were waiting to take the lead from him. In their eyes there was a gleam of hope of a possible surrender, of giving up the struggle. A flash of desperate, impossible hope was there for a moment and was gone.

Aldo Puglisi understood it. He read it clearly in their eyes just as they read it in his, because they shared the same hope and the same despair. He crumpled the leaflet in his fist, looking in front of him at the sea.

'Do you really believe that they would let us get away alive?' he said. Gerace shook his head. He was thinking of what had happened on Santa Maura.

No, no one believed the fluttering message of the Germans. They knew quite well that the Germans were just preparing another trap and that the only way that they could save themselves was to fight on, defeat and disarm the powerful garrison at Lixourion, to go on fighting in spite of the Stukas and the dive bombers. And perhaps, at any moment an Anglo-American or Italian force might be seen approaching from the sea. Somewhere there must still have been ships of the Royal Italian Navy. The wireless station in Brindisi continued to encourage the division to fight on. It praised the command and the soldiers of the division for what they had done. Badoglio's government and the Allies could not abandon them there in the middle of the sea. A small naval squadron or a few aeroplanes would be enough to change the outcome

149

of the fighting. Or was Cefalonia too small an island, too insignificant to matter in their strategy?

It was too small an island and one of absolutely no importance to their plans. The general turned to look at it, on the map hanging on the wall. Cefalonia was hardly more than a rock, far removed from the battle fronts and from any useful shipping route.

It was certainly of no value to the Allies, and he knew it.

He wondered where at that moment the sub-lieutenant was who had left during the night with a hospital ship. It had been the last boat remaining in Argostolion and he wondered if, escaping the vigilance of the German patrols, it had crossed the straits of Otranto and reached Brindisi safely. Once there, the naval officer would have been able to make clear the position on Cefalonia and the predicament of the division. But what use would that be?

He placed his hands on the windowsill. He looked out at the last of the leaflets which the wind was scattering on to the ruined houses in the town, fluttering around the palm trees in Piazza Valianos.

Supporter of Badoglio, he thought, the destiny of the nation, the German comrades. Words, meaningless words, or with a meaning distorted, or words capable of distorting the truth. Now, he thought, from one day to the next the truth could become the opposite of what it had been.

There was another sort of truth, small but cogent, with bearing on the immediate course of events; if the division were to surrender not one of them would live to tell the tale.

2

The sea was an uneasy, undisputed road for the two battalions, under the command of Major von Hirchfeld, from the first German Alpine Division which disembarked in the bay at Kiriaki during the nights of the 18th and 19th of September. According to Colonel Barge's reckoning, air support alone would not be enough to enable the garrison at Lixourion to break the resistance of the Italian division. Reinforcements of men were necessary to enable a completely successful offensive to be mounted. Picked troops, trained for mountainous conditions, such as existed on the island, were required.

Major von Hirchfeld's men disembarked. It was another moonlit night. The waters of the bay of Kiriaki glittered as they lapped gently along the sides of the boats. The pine-woods on the mountain bathed in moonlight came down to the sea and were lost in it.

The boats drew into the shore. Words of command resounded sharp and clear. Even a whisper sounded like a shout in the crystalline air of the moonlit night. The dry sound of the boats' sides against the rocks, the footsteps of the first troops to jump ashore, the sound of the battalions forming up under the wall of the mountain, were clearly heard.

The engines of the launches died away. The surface of the bay which had been broken by the bows of the boats recomposed itself into immobility. But the air had lost its scent of woods, damp grass, and sun-baked earth and rocks still warm in the chill of the night. The sparkling air in the amphitheatre of Kiriaki was absorbing the odours of the two battalions.

Beneath the wall of the mountain the two battalions came to life. They moved off in column along the white, moonlit road. They went towards the faint undulating line of the mountains of Cefalonia; mountains which were their natural element. Without songs, shouts or words of command the alpine troops made off towards their positions, giving their rhythm to the night.

It was not a rhythm that recalled distant mountains and valleys, other nights and other moons, but a hard silent rhythm of war that made the men move like self-propelled machines, like death-dealing automata that nothing would be able to stop.

151

On the morning of the attack Karl Ritter had the feeling of having seen it all before, of reliving an experience that he had already had, of a repetition of gestures and actions made somewhere else.

It was not only a sensation; it was an actual fact; one countryside was like another. There was a house in the middle of a wood, a woman by the roadside, a voice. Enough to throw him giddily backwards into the past.

He took a drink of water from a spring, raised his hand to give the signal to advance, and moved off under a still-dark sky. All this he had done before.

The mill to the left, the path, the damp grass in the wood, the mountains drawing nearer, spread out under the clear light of the stars; and the presence of an enemy all round him ready to strike: it had happened innumerable other times.

Complete concentration was necessary all the time, eyes staring into the dark, ears straining, even noses sniffing to catch the scent of the enemy so as not to be caught unawares, so as to be the first to kill. It was like a hunting party.

A hunting party or even a sports meeting of mortal character, with a plan to be regulated by the fluorescent face of a chronometer.

The brilliance of the stars was losing its intensity. Towards the east of the island the sky was growing pale. The peak of Dafni stood out more and more clearly, sharp and dark against the growing light, but amongst the pines and olive groves on its slopes the path climbed up indistinctly, in a confusing pattern of light and shadow.

'Oberleutnant,' a low voice called out. He stopped and the column halted. He went forward across the damp carpet beneath the pines and saw on the other side of the road, below a cultivated terrace, the Italian camp. It was pitched in the middle of an olive grove and from above it looked small and compact. The field kitchen was lined up at the edge of the clearing. A vague mass of animals, indistinguishable from there, was sleeping, motionless as though sculpted, under the trees.

Karl Ritter made a sign, a wave of his hand in the green air of the wood, and this was enough to make his men fan out rapidly around him as though they had sprung up out of the grass.

Two sentries were walking up and down the road near the tents of the camp. They stopped to talk, but their voices could not be heard. They were smoking, their rifles slung on their backs. They sat down on the edge of the road and went on talking as they looked at the light of daybreak rising up from Zante.

Karl Ritter was kneeling on the grass. He drew a deep breath. He was about to give the signal to attack. Now it was a question of playing a game of cunning, of transforming oneself as far as possible into a hunting animal. The accumulation of hate must not be released without thought, it must be calculatingly mastered and transformed into energy and battle skill.

He got up, stretched his arm in front of him softly without violence as though to pluck something invisible from the air. He moved down the slope of the hill almost sliding, his machine pistol held in front of him at the level of his belt, aware of a well-controlled landslide of boots, faces and weapons on either side of him and behind. It was a moving wall of iron that slid with him and bore down on the tents of the enemy.

He saw the faces of the sentries as they turned at the noise from the pine trees. He was able to recognize first their surprise and then the fear which wiped out the sleepiness of the night. It seemed to him that they turned to shout out something and that they opened their mouths to cry out, but he did not give them the time for it. He fired. His men opened fire as they slithered into the area of the camp. The first things to move were the mules tethered by the legs to the olive trees. They pawed the ground, dragging at their ropes. Shouts and voices disturbed the grey tents that loomed out of the shadows. The camp echoed with cries and curses. Soldiers appeared

153

at the opening of their tents and fell flat on their faces. Some tottered, half-dressed, their hair on end, their eyes staring, reeling with their hands stretched out in front of them as if they were searching for support. They fell, rolled on the ground, and remained motionless, with their eyes reflecting the branches of the trees.

Some raised their hands to the sky, but Karl Ritter and his men went on firing, bent low, running along the paths between the tents, shooting at everything that moved, as though bewitched by the very flames that spurted from their guns.

'Stop, stop!' The officer commanding the camp appeared in front of the Germans on the edge of the terrace, with his hands raised, shouting something. It would have been easy to shoot him there, exposed as he was. Karl Ritter stopped, and his soldiers became motionless, their weapons ready in their hands. The smell of hot metal once again filled the air, stronger than the smell of the trees and mules.

The Italians surrendered. The enemy gathered round their commander, and all of them gave themselves up with their hands raised in the growing light of dawn.

And this too, the surrender of the enemy, had happened at other times before. He had witnessed it before at the end of a fight, in the returning stillness of the mountains or plain. The faces of the enemy became again those of ordinary men, dark-eyed and dazed or fearful and exhausted, for the most part unshaven, with the silence of defeat on their lips. But these faces were also the faces of their former comrades, not just of an ordinary enemy; the lowest down the scale of enemies; the worst enemy; more hostile even than the British, Americans, Russians or Greeks. They were an enemy placed beyond the rules of war. Did the Italian commander and his men realize their position? Did they realize the treachery of the stab in the back they had given the Germans? Or were they hoping that by raising their hands in the air, making a simple, internationally recognized gesture, they were going to succeed in wiping out their shame and save their skins?

Saving their skins, that was all that mattered to the

Italians. But this time the game was going to be played rather differently from the way it had been on other occasions. This time there were not going to be any prisoners.

He made them march off on the Dafni road, the officers in front and behind them their battered men, with their puttees falling round their ankles, or with bare feet slopping loosely in their boots, some without jackets, some in vests without their shirts, and some with bare chests. They were mule drivers who would not have known how to put up a fight for a minute even if they had had a warning of the attack.

He spat on the road and took a gulp from his water bottle; it was warm, not cold like the spring. He was thirsty. His mouth felt as though it was full of dust. He looked at his wristwatch; it was six o'clock. On the other side of the island the sun was sliding up out of the sea. The ridge of Dafni on the opposite slope was lit up and the reflection overflowed on to the south side brightening the road, below which a long narrow ditch opened in the rocky, heather-covered soil. Its bottom was lost to view. Karl Ritter gave the order to halt. The prisoners were in a good position on the bend of the curve. Fire from either end of the column would cross on them, and the bodies could easily be pushed into the ditch.

Karl Ritter opened fire first. For the second time there was an expression of surprise on the faces of the prisoners, but not for long. Officers and men fell on top of one another. They stumbled over one another in a useless attempt to escape, they tripped and fell. There were screams and cries. But then once again the silence of the pines prevailed and the Germans hurriedly cleared the road. The column resumed its march, climbing up towards the summit of Dafni.

According to the battle plan, it was up there that the objective lay that had to be destroyed. By eight o'clock sharp he had to join up with the three columns of Major von Hirchfeld's alpine troops which at that moment ought to have been advancing along the valley of Kuzuli, and sweep away any possible nests of Italian resistance.

The road deteriorated into a mule track winding its way up with sudden turns and steep slopes between the thinning pines, brambles and clumps of yellow flowered broom. Adjusting his binoculars Karl Ritter slowly swept the broken crest of Dafni. It was so close that the Italians seemed to be within an arm's length. The soldiers of the 317th Regiment were moving about their positions smiling, chatting casually as though they were at home.

He moved forward towards the clearing on the crest which was almost completely unprotected, motioning his men to spread out in a straight line so that they could roll into the clearing like a wave. He fired a long burst towards the summit. The valley threw back the sound and it echoed away in the distance. There was no reply from the Italians. Voices were heard. The panic and the terror could be imagined. Karl Ritter stopped again, the pause before the final spring. He remained standing, completely exposed to the enemy but absolutely calm, certain that the Italians would not open fire. His men, too, were motionless, leaning forward poised to spring, their machine pistols ready, gazing at the enemy positions.

'Italians, you are surrounded,' the lieutenant shouted. His voice sounded strangely feeble under the empty sky in the open space of the clearing. He was afraid that they might not have heard him. He fired a second burst and waited until its echoes had died away. He let go his grip on his gun and put his hands round his mouth. 'Italians, you must surrender,' he yelled, 'we will give you ten minutes.'

Automatically he looked at his watch while his right hand once more found its hold on his gun. It was 7.20. Would they surrender? He was ready to swear that they would. He looked at his men drawn up for the attack and it seemed as if they too shared his conviction. Some were kneeling on the ground, some were lying face downwards, some were still standing with their heads thrust forward as though about to start a race. All seemed fully aware of their own invincible strength.

The sound of mortar fire broke out on the other side of Dafni: Major von Hirchfeld's column had reached its objective too. Karl Ritter gave a sigh of relief and a welcome feeling of relaxation filled his whole being. He felt in the pocket of his combat jacket for a cigarette. As he struck a match he glanced at his watch. It was 7.25. He inhaled deeply and looked at the tip of his cigarette. Then he saw a white flag waved by a soldier fluttering over the enemy positions. A little group of Italian officers came out to the edge of the clearing and seemed to be waiting for instructions, uneasy and uncertain.

They moved towards him. Rapidly he gave out the necessary orders to enable the operation to be finished as quickly as possible. The junction with the mountain troops must not be delayed. All the objectives had to be taken before the Stukas and Messerschmitts joined in the battle and the combined operation would start within an hour.

He drank warm water from his bottle and spat on the well trodden earth of the gun position. He did not want to listen to the Italians. What use would it have been? What could they have had to say? The grenadiers could grab the prisoners' watches and rings. The Italians were not prisoners of war, they were the spoils of victory. Never in his career as a soldier had it been his lot to fight against so useless an enemy. He put his water bottle to his lips once more and spat again on the dried up earth of the road which ran down towards the sea.

The column of grenadiers marched towards the sea which lay stretched out below the terraced olive groves. It lay dull and dead looking as the sun was still hidden from it by the chain of mountains. Only towards the horizon where the first rays of light had reached was there a ribbon of sparkling blue.

Perhaps at Farsa he would find a drinking fountain. Farsa was a pile of dark roofs on the main road to Argostolion. It was there that they would find Major von Hirchfeld's column as well as a drink of water in the village square.

An old peasant woman came to the door of her house and looked at the column of soldiers and their prisoners going down towards the sea. She said nothing, but simply stared, and from behind her black skirts the faces and wide open eyes of children peered out. Then the door was shut and the little house which looked as if it were part of the countryside

157

stood solitary in the olive groves.

The footsteps of his men on the road and those of the Italian soldiers and the way they walked seemed to him to define the different racial characteristics. The prisoners walked huddled together without discipline like a small flock of sheep. They constituted a drag and were slowing up the pace of the descent.

At Kuruklata there was a ravine by the road. It was bigger than the ditch at Dafni. There the mountains came to an end and the road followed the contours of the coast. Karl Ritter counted the Italian officers. There were eighteen. He did not count the N.C.Os or the men, but he was going to have them shot too. They were all going to be shot.

He gave orders that they were to be taken down into the ravine and shot there. After the shooting two sappers were to lay mines among the bodies and detonate them.

The Italians realized that something was going to happen and they threw themselves against their escort, shouting, and then some began to weep, calling out the names of their mothers and fathers, and of the Madonna. Karl Ritter found the spectacle unbearable. He felt ashamed for them, because they did not know how to die like men. He raged against them and against himself for having waited until they reached Kuruklata. The idea of having to see a soldier weep! This had never happened to him before.

Quickly Karl Ritter placed himself at the head of the column and gave the signal to advance before the shooting in the ravine had finished.

What could traitors expect? A surrender with full military honours?

Now the immediate objective was Farsa. On the other slope beyond Farsa the alpine troops were fighting their battle. The mortars were ploughing up the olive groves and the fields, reducing the roofs of the houses to rubble. From the countryside and from the coast Italian machine gun positions were answering the fire of the mountain troops, but what were they going to do when they realized that the column of grenadiers was taking them in the rear?

158

They must hurry to get into the engagement and throw themselves into the fight. Up till now they had only marched, surprised a detachment of mule drivers in their sleep, and accepted the surrender of an isolated battalion. Until now they had only shot defenceless men; Italians, but defenceless. Karl Ritter prayed with all his heart that Farsa might have to be taken house by house, street by street, and that the enemy might be killed fighting. He prayed too that all the enemy in the peninsula would put up a resistance so that they could be wiped out in battle.

Yes, the Italians were there beyond the wooden bridge, behind the low dark wall of stone and earth which ran along a field bounding an orchard. The Italians were firing from there.

Now, to throw himself on the ground, to surround them, overrun them, penetrate into the streets of Farsa, push on to the village square and drink a draught of fresh water.

He dropped to the ground firing at the wall, and when he leapt over it there were the Italians lying dead around their machine guns. There were dead behind the corners of the houses and at the crossroads. At last Italian soldiers were falling with weapons in their hands. Then there remained a little group of them in the middle of the square pinned down between the fire of the grenadiers and the mountain troops who had entered the village from the south.

'Kill them,' Karl Ritter shouted at his men. 'Kill them here.'

Contact had been made almost exactly as planned. Karl Ritter found the fountain and drank greedily. When he looked up to dry his mouth with the back of his hand the first squadrons of Stukas and Messerschmitts were going into action, diving on to Argostolion, on to the last of the Italian artillery positions. The battle for Cefalonia was practically finished.

4

It was all over and Adriana knew it; not from the arrival of the planes, but from the unexpected silence in the villa and all around it. The sound of distant firing had ceased and on Cefalonia there was a pause of expectation.

Where had Signora Nina and the rest of the girls run off to? Did they think by doing that they could escape their fate?

Adriana did not move, nor did she look out. The shutters were closed. A soft green light filtered through the slats and fell like knife blades on the carpet and the tiles. The smoke from a cigarette in the ash tray sent a thin straight thread towards the ceiling. 'Here come the Stukas again,' she thought to herself.

The villa shook. The last of the windows shattered in a nearby room. A door blew open and shut and a blast of hot air swept into the room. The thread of smoke was broken and dissipated.

Automatically Adriana stretched out for her half-smoked cigarette. She stopped her hand in mid air and looked at it carefully. It was, she noticed, a poor thin discoloured hand, with lifeless nails, and a thousand little parchment-like wrinkles. For years, for eternity it had been dispensing caresses for cash payment without receiving anything in exchange, except the weary life of lodging houses. 'Never a little real love in exchange,' thought Adriana. Once again she cast her mind back over her years of selling love, but she could not succeed in remembering one single face that stood out from the nameless crowd, nor could she remember the name of even one of them.

The Stukas came in low over the road. They seemed to be right above the garden wall. A blast of air burst open the shutters and the light of day poured into the room. Adriana jumped from the bed and went to shut them. As she did so, dazzled by the light, she saw the black wings of the plane rush in towards her as though it was she, Adriana, that was its prey and no one else. A burst of machine gun fire tore through the soil of the garden and made off with the shadow of the plane. Adriana thought that it might after all have been better to make for the pinewoods with Signora Nina and the girls.

Fear was joined by weariness and resignation. Then to the awareness of death at first accepted with despair was added terror and rebellion. She must not, she could not die like this. She had nothing to do with the war.

It was not fair. It was not written in her contract, she thought desperately, and tears of impotence welled from her eyes. It was through these tears that she saw the black wing of a plane swooping once more on the garden, touching it lightly with a long caress.

It was not in the contract, she thought. But this was not the time to go into what contract had been broken. The caress, falling from the wings, passed over her and swept on beyond the walls and roofs of the villa, and reached the road on the hill.

5

At 11.00 hours on September 22nd, after the three columns of Major von Hirchfeld's alpine troops and Oberleutnant Karl Ritter's grenadiers had brought their action to a close and had surrounded and eliminated the last nest of Italian resistance; after the Stukas and the Messerschmitts had knocked out the artillery positions; after, or so it was said, two Italian warships that had appeared on the horizon had been driven off by German aircraft; at 11.00 hours on 22nd September, the white flag was raised on the tower of the Italian headquarters in Argostolion.

The white flag fluttered above the town in a sky free from aeroplanes and shells. It flew above a confused babble of voices, the shouts of men and women who came out from shelter amongst the pinewoods and the olive groves to see again the miracle of a clear sky, and the sad sight of the columns of prisoners escorted by their captors marching towards the villages, the market places and the barracks at Argostolion, amidst the dust thrown up by the motorcyclists and tanks.

Karl Ritter sat down. His legs felt heavy with weariness. Exhaustion always overcame him when a battle was over. He had marched for miles between the hills of Cefalonia and the sea. He had been marching since the dawn of the day before. He had travelled for so long that even now, seated on a dusty bench in Piazza Valianos, the ground before his eyes seemed to go on passing beneath him, with the undulating movement of the march.

He lit his last cigarette, and threw the packet on the broken paving of the piazza. But he could not taste the flavour of the tobacco. His mouth was burning.

His eyes too were burning from the brilliant light of the day and from the darkness that had surrounded him all night. But most of all he felt an inner burning, which set fire to every atom of his body. It was the long thirst of battle, unquenchable here just as in France, Yugoslavia, Russia, Africa, everywhere. The thirst, united with exhaustion and lack of sleep, which went on even after the battle.

He looked at the white flag above him. He looked at Piazza Valianos which stretched around him, battered by the bombardment. The asphalt of the roadway was broken. A crater, almost perfectly round, laid bare the earth beneath the layers of hardcore. The buildings on either side of the piazza including the cafés were in ruins or badly damaged. In the two flower beds by the bench clumps of soft orange coloured dahlias stood untouched in spite of their fragility, miraculously clean amidst all the dust from the rubble. Karl's exhausted eyes fell upon them in surprise. He stretched out his hand and picked one. He held it in the palm of his hand and gazed at it.

How many of them had they killed? He did not know. Perhaps a hundred or so. He had been marching through the smoke-filled villages of Cefalonia since the dawn of the day before. Dafni, Kuruklata, Farsa; nests of machine guns destroyed, artillery positions overrun, infantry wiped out between the walls of farm houses, behind churches, in woods, in olive groves, or shot down in the middle of village squares.

How many had they shot? Karl threw away the flower. He had rested long enough. He must get up. His men had been resting, too. They were sitting on the ground close by and

162

had finished eating. Some were smoking and some talking, but for the most part they kept silent, absorbed, as though their minds were far away.

It was a pity that in this moment of victory he should be overcome by this deathly tiredness, the stupefying morning light, burning thirst, and sleep. Karl could not remember ever having enjoyed a victory to the full or having savoured all its fruits. Victories always came unexpectedly when physical endurance had reached its limit and conscious reason had given way.

He must get up from the bench and move across the broken paving of the piazza. His men, who were in danger of falling asleep, must be called together. He must find Major von Hirchfeld and discover exactly what were his next orders, where he was to go, what he was to do, and how many more of them were to be shot. He must learn from Major von Hirchfeld whether, now that they had hoisted the white flag, the shooting would still have to go on.

But he continued sitting with his arms stretched along the back of the seat, his eyes moving between the white flag and the columns of Italian prisoners who on foot and in lorries were being taken along the seafront to the naval barracks. They were looking at him, as though they wanted to arouse his sympathy and beg his pardon, as though they wanted him to understand that they had been guiltless.

They were the same eyes that had been looking at him since the dawn of the preceding day. They were the eyes of humbled men, ashamed of themselves, of men with their backs to a wall, forced to look at death itself. It was the look with which a wounded animal tries to convey something, when no other means of expression exists.

It was the look of the prisoners caught and shot on Dafni, at Farsa, and further on at Procopata and on the road to Argostolion.

How many had been shot with that look of astonishment and sudden recognition of death on their faces? They had only their bare hands, unbuttoned tunics and open shirts to protect themselves from the bursts of machine gun fire, and as they fell they had put their bare hands over their eyes as though to avoid the sight of the face of death.

He dragged himself to his feet. He must make the effort to find Major von Hirchfeld, or anyway, someone to give him orders. Perhaps his task was finished with the end of the fighting. He walked across the piazza which had stopped heaving up and down as it had done when he had first got to his feet. His men got up too, with a dry sound as their equipment dropped into place around them. Automatically they fell in behind him ready to take to the road again towards whatever objective they were ordered, uninterested and weary though they might be. He looked at them, his splendid men. Their eyes were serene in spite of the redness from lack of sleep. They had destroyed, burned, killed, and passed through yet another battle. Now once again there they were, after a rest, ready to move on. A biscuit, a piece of chocolate was enough to recharge their energy. They were leaving behind them hundreds of dead.

He turned his gaze from the sun and battle blackened faces of his soldiers and saw a small column of vehicles rapidly approaching on the road from Kerameis which ran along the hill close above the broken roofs. It approached and grew bigger until he could make out an officer from the alpine battalion at the head of the column and behind him in another vehicle the Italian divisional commander. Other vehicles filled with Italian officers followed in a cloud of dust, and bringing up the rear in a truck were German soldiers armed with machine guns.

The convoy slowed down and entered the piazza accompanied by the cloud of dust which had followed it down the eucalyptus avenue. The German officers jumped to the ground followed by the alpine troops. They formed up on either side of the headquarters with their machine guns at the ready. The Italian general and his officers got down. They seemed a little bemused to find themselves at their own headquarters as prisoners. The general moved towards the entrance preceded and followed by German officers. He was going up to his office to sign the surrender, an unconditional surrender, thought Karl Ritter.

The rest of the Italian officers remained outside, leaning against the wings of the trucks, a handful of survivors, Karl Ritter concluded, frightened and uncertain, reduced to the level of their men.

He moved to the edge of the piazza near the convoy and looked at them carefully. Yes, his friend the captain was amongst the survivors. Aldo Puglisi had escaped death and was there leaning against the door of a staff car. He had no belt, his tunic was crumpled and he was looking blankly down the eucalyptus avenue where the dust was settling. He seemed to be waiting, but without much conviction or even much desire, for someone who might come down the avenue.

The townspeople who had fled to the hills were returning down the avenue. They were hesitant and were asking each other if the war between the Italians and the Germans was really over. They watched the sky fearfully lest the aeroplanes might return. They looked at the ruins of their town, without a word, as though they were prepared for the sight that awaited them. They looked in silence at the prisoners, their Italian friends, and at the German soldiers. Karl Ritter felt that they had got what they deserved for being friends with the Italians.

Suddenly Aldo Puglisi turned his head and looked at Karl Ritter. He looked at him steadily leaning his back against the door of his vehicle. His face was expressionless. There was neither resentment nor hate, nor even any desire to ask forgiveness. No, he just looked at him, with the air of not seeing him. His gaze went through him to something further away. It was a look devoid of warmth, cold and remote, like the gaze of a dead man.

6

He was seeing the road at Kerameis which was like all the roads of the island, running through olive groves and woods, with a stone kerb at its edge and a bridge over a dried up stream. He saw the villa where the tactical headquarters of the division and the artillery command had withdrawn to organize the final attempt at resistance. It was a villa like so many on the island, unpretentious, a yellowish colour, with dusty shutters and a turret which gave a view of the hills and valleys. He saw the general standing in the doorway of his last command post in front of a parched garden awaiting the Germans and he saw the white flag on the turret.

He saw two soldiers on the road coming towards the villa, reeling as if they were drunk. They had told them quite quietly, with the calmness of madmen, that up there at Trojanata the German alpine troops were shooting the prisoners.

'And they shot us, too. Don't you believe me?'

'Yes, we have been shot, too. I am not joking, look here, look at my wound still bleeding. Can't you see it?'

He heard again their voices, almost matter of fact, as though they were talking about a misfortune that had happened to someone else.

'Go on, look at my wound; the bullet went right through my arm, in one side and out the other. I am not being funny. Feel my arm, go on, feel it.'

He saw again the broken arm, hanging limp, and the blood, and the madness which smouldered in their eyes.

'They are coming down here, you know.'

'That's right. It is all over at Trojanata. They're all dead; shot. We were shot, too.'

'They'll be here in a little while and you will see it with your own eyes.'

'In a little while we shall all be dead. We shall all be shot here, too.'

Up in the turret of the villa he had waited for the Germans with his field glasses trained on the road which came down from Trojanata and Castro. They had appeared indistinctly in the distance after they had driven the Italians out of Castro. They advanced through the smoke of fires, as though they were coming through a fog. Little by little the sun had risen on the woods and the line of their advance had become clearer.

The Italians had preceded them by a few miles in a solid unbroken column; cars, tanks, horses, mules, field kitchens, guns, troop carriers. The column had moved along the road with the slow irresistible forward movement of a wall of lava. But when the squadrons of Stukas appeared in the sky, it had split and burst apart. The men fled. The little Stukas fell upon them and ferreted them out amongst the olive groves, machine gunning them and blowing them to pieces.

He saw once more the livingroom on the first floor of the villa where the general had called his last order group together; the dark leather armchair, and a grandfather clock against the wall between the windows which looked out on to a garden. A big map of the island had been spread out on the table in the middle of the room and the general's hand had indicated names and locations. He had his back to a bookcase with its shelves half empty and on a small table there was a photograph of a young woman at the wheel of an open car.

He saw all this again in every detail. It surprised him that at the moment when the decision to surrender the division had been taken he should have noticed such unimportant things; a button missing from a colonel's tunic, a tear in the sleeve of another tunic, the beard of a colleague red like a burst of flame, things which at other times he would never have noticed. The voice of the general had sounded unreal and out of place in the midst of these trivial details.

There remained nothing to do but to surrender. The plans which headquarters had made to hold the German attack had been upset by the aeroplanes and defeated by the landing of the mountain troops. Communication between unit and unit, and units and headquarters, had been lost.

No, there remained nothing else to be done, and once more he saw the missing button, the torn sleeve, the grandfather clock whose hands had stopped who knew how long ago, at twenty-four minutes past nine.

Then the general had left them but they pressed round him and followed him to the doorway and into the garden, little bigger than Katerina Pariotis' garden. They had waited for the arrival of the Germans. Finally he remembered a soldier climbing up the turret to hoist the white flag.

Without much hope he wondered if Gerace might have succeeded in hiding in his Greek girl's house and if others of his men might have escaped captivity in the same way.

Would it be captivity? he wondered.

He consoled himself with the thought that he too had a Greek girl who would have hidden him in case of need. But how could he escape the vigilance of the German guards and get to her?

He thought of the dark eyes of Katerina and Amalia, the little wooden room with a picture of Aghios Nicolaos at the head of the bed and the window looking out on to the freshness of the orchard. He thought, too, of the bedroom at home so far away beyond the sea, which he shared with his wife. It no longer seemed to exist. There he had a son who must just be starting to walk.

Perhaps none of this really existed and the whole thing was a dream; the voices, the faces, the rooms. Perhaps only his torn uniform had been and continued to be real.

CHAPTER NINETEEN

1

DURING THE NIGHT the fires were lit. The first and biggest burst out on the hills over Trojanata. In the white glare of burning petrol the roofs of the village huddled round the tower of the church and the road and the olive groves suddenly appeared.

Other smaller fires burnt in the valley at Santa Barbara which opened deep beneath the mass of Enos. There were fires at Kardakata, Kuruklata and in other unidentified places near Dafni. They flared up one after the other as though started by flying sparks.

The last fire appeared on the opposite side of the island in the misty darkness of Sant' Eufemia, by the narrow neck of sea five miles wide which separated Ithaca from Cefalonia.

The island of Ithaca remained wrapped in its classical silence. Its inhabitants watched from their houses and the countryside, repeating to each other the incredible tales spread around the island by a Cefaliot fisherman who had come over from Sami.

'What are they doing?' they asked each other, filled with curiosity and fear. 'What are they trying to do?'

The people of Cefalonia were asking themselves the same question. From their windows shuttered against the night they peered out at the German troops, listened to their voices and shouts and to the sound of their footsteps drawing near and dying away along the tracks and roads of the island. They heard the sound of horses' hooves and vehicles. They saw the vague outlines of soldiers carrying unidentifiable burdens on their backs. But as soon as the fires were lit, the figures stood out clearly, activated as though by madness, hurling

169

petrol from cans on to the fires so that the flames might keep burning. Then the soldiers on foot made off carrying away the empty cans. Cavalry patrols came and went slowly, tall and dark against the white light of the fires.

'They are burning the Italian soldiers,' the islanders said to each other. 'They've shot them and now they are burning them so that no one will ever be able to find any trace of them, so that no one in the world will ever know anything about it.'

Then even the cavalry detachments that had been patrolling round the pyres withdrew and the sound of their horses' hooves died away on the roads leading back to their camps. In the silence of the night no longer broken by machine gun or artillery fire or by German planes, the Cefaliots listened to the merry, dry crackling of the fires.

Here and there men and women came out of their houses. Uncertainly they made their way towards the fires. They went not by the paths or roads but across the hard dry earth of the fields parched by the drought of summer, and through the olive groves and woods. A few Italian soldiers who had found safety in the peasants' houses came out with them and were dazed at finding themselves once more in the midst of living people, able to walk, run and feel the ground beneath their feet and to see the stars in the sky above their heads. To them even the bright light amongst the trees seemed beautiful.

They approached along ditches and irrigation canals. As they drew slowly nearer, the crackling of the flames grew into a roar, no longer merry; a long moaning lament. The smell of burning petrol carried a hint of resin, olive wood and pine wood. But they smelt something else too, which added something new to the scent of burning oil and wood, something bitter sweet and sickly.

The flames lit up their surroundings as bright as day. They advanced quickly on a solid front, all the time engulfing more and more corpses. Some lay on their backs or face downwards, their arms flung wide, lying by their sides, or crossed on their chests. Heads lay to one side or thrown back in strange, unnatural positions.

The men and women of Cefalonia, peasants, seafarers,

fishermen, foresters, with the few Italian soldiers who had escaped the shooting, looked at them. For a long moment they remained motionless at the edge of the brightly lit areas asking themselves how many corpses there were in the pyre that burned before them. How many of them had they known, with how many of them had they talked, how many friends had been butchered and burnt? Or they remained silent, just looking on in horror.

Then some of them went up to the bodies not yet touched by the flames and carried away as many as they could across their shoulders, or with one taking the feet and another the head. They loaded them on carts, where there were still carts that could be used. Each one went away from the German holocaust carrying a dead man to save him from destruction, and trudged wearily along the spine of the hill in search of a suitable burying place. Some of the bodies were placed in mountain grottoes, damp places whose walls dripped with water. Some were lowered into cisterns amongst the fields and vines and some buried in great communal graves.

The Cefaliots and the survivors of the division dug graves until the first light of dawn; they went up and down from ditch to pyre, from pyre to cistern and grotto until the sky above Zante began to pale. Then, afraid lest the alpine troops and the grenadiers might reappear on the island's roads, they withdrew to their homes and hid in their houses.

They shut themselves in, but for a long time their eyes still saw the vision of the fires, the waxen faces of the dead, the vacant glassy stares, and from their houses they continued to gaze out at the distant flames until the light of the sun burst over Cefalonia and dimmed them.

In the daylight the fires disappeared but the smoke, thick dirty clouds, could be seen.

That smoke, the Cefaliots and the survivors thought, that smoke, the Italian officers who had been taken prisoner and shut up in the Mussolini Barracks on the seafront at Argostolion thought, was the Acqui Division rising up into the sky.

How many, they wondered, how many of them had been burnt? 146 officers and 4,000 men, taken alive and then killed in the summary executions, rose up towards the sky in that thick, dirty cloud of smoke. But no one in Cefalonia, not even Major von Hirchfeld or Colonel Barge, would have been able to say the exact numbers.

They looked at the smoke, each one asking himself the same question.

'And we, only we, have survived to tell the tale,' Aldo Puglisi thought bitterly from the window of the barracks.

Leaning his hands on the windowsill, he looked out at the island, which once again was opening its arms round the bay to the fresh light of yet another morning, miraculous and unexpected.

He thought with bitterness of the cruelty of fate that had decreed death for so many of them and the safety of prison for him. They had learnt the previous evening from an alpine officer that they were safe. That morning at half past seven, they were to be taken to Sami and there embarked for Patras and sent to concentration camps. All those clouds in the sky had been necessary to placate the fury of the Germans and to satisfy their thirst for vengeance.

Voices and footsteps were heard along the barrack passages. Aldo Puglisi looked at his watch. The Germans were coming to take them away. It was exactly half past seven.

Four troop carriers of the Wehrmacht were parked on the seafront in front of the Mussolini Barracks and German soldiers in combat dress were waiting.

The sea! The sea stretched beyond the harbour, beyond the bridge. It was the same sea as always, the same intense blue as it always was at that hour of the morning.

Groups of people had collected here and there on the seafront to see them, but the journey from the barrack gate to the troop carriers was short. The soldiers of the escort drawn up in two files did not allow the curious to see much.

They climbed up into the vehicles, giving each other a helping hand, happy to breathe the clean sea air after a night of waiting in the barracks.

The general had been taken away before them. He had been driven off towards Sami. At this moment his vehicle and its escort should be approaching Sami or in sight of Sami.

There were girls, old men, babies, in the groups that had collected on the seafront. Women had come to say goodbye to their Italian boyfriends, and to see them for the last time. Aldo Puglisi scanned the faces but Katerina Pariotis was not there. He would have liked to have written to her, to tell her what he had in his heart, what it would have been fitting to say before he went away. Once again he would have asked her forgiveness for everything; for having come to Cefalonia in the guise of a conqueror; for having wished well of her and perhaps having made her suffer a little. This time she would have to forgive him too, for going away like this without saying goodbye to her.

He would remember Katerina Pariotis for ever, the little, dark, thin girl; the hostile girl who little by little had become his friend once she had understood that there was no enemy, that the enemy did not exist in any man or any place. Could he ever have been the enemy of anyone in spite of all the uniforms; he, Aldo Puglisi, or his artillerymen?

The troop carriers moved off. Two trucks filled with an escort led the way and brought up the rear of the short column. The hands of the onlookers rose in the air in gestures of farewell. The officers waved back. The convoy went along the seafront, turned to the left, re-entered the town and came out into the clearing of Piazza Valianos. The white flag still fluttered over the headquarters. No one had bothered to haul it down. Other townspeople were moving about the ruins with a stunned air. Aldo Puglisi saw the piazza for the last time and felt himself overcome by sadness, the melancholy of parting. He thought he saw Nicolino amongst the crowd which became motionless as they passed, and seated on a suitcase unbelievably elegant and unreal in her black dress was Signora Nina surrounded by her girls. They too looked on in silence as the officers passed by, prisoners, scarcely moving their hands in a timid salute. Perhaps the girls envied their departure.

Who would worry himself now about the fate of the poor girls? wondered Aldo Puglisi.

Signora Nina had jumped to her feet shouting something and waving her long arms, but amidst the noise of the troop carriers she seemed to be shouting without sound. He recognised La Triestina, who had gone to her side to calm her.

The column went on. Instead of turning into Via Principe di Piemonte towards the bridge across the bay and then turning on to the Sami road, the radiators pointed in the direction of the eucalyptus avenue, and passed down it gradually increasing speed. Argostolion, the bridge, and the Sami road were left behind. They drove along the coast road to San Teodoro.

'Where are we going?' someone asked. 'Where are they taking us?'

Aldo Puglisi saw the familiar trees, the villas and the gardens. Round the bend he would see Katerina's house and then the sea mills, the lighthouse and the stretch of beach where he used to go to bathe with her, and where he had been, too, with Oberleutnant Ritter. Katerina's house passed in a flash. It came towards them and was left behind in a moment. The shutters were closed, the little garden bursting with flowers was deserted. Katerina was probably asleep. Perhaps she too had been up all night watching the fires. He might have known that they would have been brought this way. He should have written a farewell note and thrown it into the garden tied to a stone as they passed the house.

He smiled, surprised at these childish thoughts.

But where were the Germans taking them?

The road ran along beside the sea. Great clumps of aloes standing out against the sky, on the shore and on the slope of the hills, filled the air with a subtle fragrance. On the front of a villa, red bricks against the green and silver of the olives, and on the wall that ran round the garden, bougainvillea flowering.

'What are they thinking about?' someone asked him.

But there was nothing to think about. Aldo Puglisi wondered at the simplicity of the question. They were loaded into German troop carriers and it did not matter where they went. They would get somewhere but it made no difference where.

The convoy stopped by the gate of the villa. The German soldiers posted themselves by the sides of the vehicles gripping their machine guns and pistols. They signed with the barrels of their weapons for the officers to get down. They jumped to the ground in silence and were made to go, not into the garden of the villa, but into the field alongside it.

It looked down on the Mediterranean in the morning light. It was half past eight. The white lighthouse glittered in the sun beneath the wheeling flight of the gulls which swooped and rose over the sea in an endless game.

Aldo Puglisi looked at the horizon which disappeared in a mist of light. He turned his head towards the execution squad which, drawn up opposite the wall, was waiting for them.

'This then,' he thought, 'is when I die.' The appetite for revenge was still not sated.

Resigned, strangely calm, not sad or frightened, he placed his back against the wall. Others around him fell to their knees on the dry grass of the field, asking to be confessed. A chaplain who was among the prisoners ran towards the kneeling officers and then towards the Germans shouting that international law, international law . . .

He heard his voice but he did not catch the words that followed, nor the reply of the German officer. What were the chaplain and the German talking about? They were putting off the moment. Did not they realize that they were all already dead? That there was nothing that could be done to prevent their death?

He looked towards the sea which disappeared into the distance and thought how it ran on and on from continent to continent, island to island, and that tomorrow perhaps the little waves that were lapping this beach would reach the shores of Italy.

Suddenly, as though a long way off, he felt the silence, and in the silence he heard the bursts of gunfire, but faintly and far away. He had time to be surprised that the noise was hardly noticeable. A wave of heat rose up into his mouth and darkness fell.

175

The idea of death was acceptable only with weapons in one's hands with which to fight against it. Oberleutnant Ritter understood this even though many of the Italians, the ex-general and the ex-captain Puglisi amongst them, had fallen to the weapons of his grenadiers without a word of fear or lamentation. They had been dead before his men had opened fire. At the moment when they had reached the wall, upright and silent, they had crossed the narrow threshold that separates life from death. There, against the wall, with their eyes quite vacant, they had abandoned their bodies, still untouched, and had crossed over alone into the world of the dead. Others had rebelled against the idea of death with tears and prayers.

It was not these who worried him, but those who were already dead. Not the shouts of desperation, the prayers, the names repeated as in a delirium by the prisoners kneeling or prostrate on the ground, but the necessity of shooting the dead.

The sun was up over the pinewood. He looked at his watch. It was ten fifteen. He had been shooting for more than two hours.

No, this was not fighting. This was no battle. They were not even the enemy, these men who were lined up defenceless, with their backs against the wall, their eyes filled with terror, or complete, calm indifference.

Karl Ritter lowered his gun. Why did not someone get rid of the chaplain with his black cross raised against the sky. Why had he not given the order to his men to shoot him together with the rest?

Other trucks arrived. More officers got down on to the road and came into the field. He must keep on firing as quickly as he could, but why was it just when it seemed that the executions were finished, the sound of other trucks was heard from Argostolion. How many of these Italians were there?

He gave the order to fire. The prisoners fell on top of each other writhing. Some came forward a pace surging towards the pointing gun barrels.

Now he felt completely weary. Not the healthy exhaustion after a battle, but a deathly tiredness, that made him feel that he, too, was one of the executed.

'Italians! If any of you are still alive, get up. Don't be afraid. It is all over.'

The voice of an alpine N.C.O. rang out each time loud and clear in the silence. He moved cautiously, taking care not to trample on the corpses, looking at the ground, his Luger in his right hand. He cried out his ritual formula each time with the same intonation, not addressed to anyone in particular, but to the wind, the sea, and the olive trees.

'Italians!'

If any one amongst the dead gave any sign of being only wounded, raising a hand, moving, turning a head or trying in any way to attract attention, the N.C.O. moved quickly to him and bending down pointed his Luger at the back of his neck and completed the execution.

The bodies were dragged from beyond the garden wall and dumped in the sea wells or in a big natural ditch worn in the limestone rock. This could hold about a hundred and was nearest, making the shortest journey from the place of execution. It was there that the soldiers dragged the first bodies.

'Italians! If any of you . . .'

Karl Ritter looked down the road. He had heard another convoy of prisoners approaching. A long streak of dust in the air at the edge of the pinewood marked its progress. He sat on the low wall which separated the field from the sea. These walls, he noticed, were all alike. He had seen them all over Greece and in the south of Italy too. One was like another, just as one olive tree was like another, in Cefalonia or in Greece. The dead, too, he thought, were all alike. When they fell to the ground one man was just like the next. Indeed, deprived of their different voices, they all became the same man, with the same face and the same eyes.

More prisoners were being set down and now the same scene of fear, supplication or calm indifference would begin

177

again with the chaplain in the middle of it with his cross raised in the air to give comfort and to say the prayers. There would be more fountain pens, more gold watches, more gold rings to be taken off the prisoners before they were shot. Above all there would be the moment of truth, the crossing over the threshold between life and death, and these dead, already dead standing up with their back to the wall, would have to be shot.

They got down from the troop carriers and walked across the meadow. They took in the reality of their destination without question or had they already guessed it before they had arrived?

They gazed around them with an air of bewilderment. Some sat themselves down at the foot of an olive tree, others near the blood spattered wall. They looked around or stared at the sea, motionless and unchanging in front of them. They handed over their watches and rings to the grenadiers and mountain troops without protest, though one officer threw his watch on the earth and ground his heel on it to smash it, looking in the face of the German soldier with defiance, rather than give it him.

'What are you waiting for?' someone shouted.

Again the sobs and amidst the sobs the invocation of the names of mothers, wives and children. The chaplain was entrusted with the photographs of families and given the addresses of homes.

'Padre, tell my children . . .'

'Padre, if one day you see her, tell her . . .'

Karl Ritter rose to his feet. What good was that futile gesture of defiance by the Italian officer? Why had he smashed his watch? What use was his watch going to be to him when he was dead, or his pen, or anything else?

He took a few steps across the hard turf of the meadow. He felt himself being overcome by anger at that useless gesture. A sudden cold fury made his stomach contract and rooted him to the spot, glaring at the prisoners.

They were waiting for him, sitting by the wall and the olive trees or standing up against the blue of the sea. They were weeping or silent, still living or already dead. They were waiting for him to give the order to open fire.

Why, he asked himself, had the Italian officer dared to defy his soldiers, himself, and the German army, by stamping on his watch? What use, he repeated to himself, was a watch to a dead man?

He could not make himself take a single step forward across the meadow. The enemy was there before him, the enemy for whom he had been searching ever since the days on the sports ground, the parades, the torchlight processions and the first battles, and now he could not move. He could not force himself to do his duty.

And it was his duty to exterminate the enemy completely, not to stop half way because he was overcome by exhaustion and because of a futile gesture of defiance. It was his duty to punish the traitors, to vindicate a betrayed alliance. It was vengeance.

It was a duty, he thought, as he felt the sweat trickle down his face and felt the gaze of the prisoners on him, certainly more difficult than facing death, but one which he must carry through to the end. He must not allow exhaustion, or anger, or the gesture of a prisoner, or living death, or eyes shedding tears, to stand in its way.

He must make a move and do something to break this ridiculous moment of hesitation which the prisoners and his own men, who waiting with their sergeant on the other side of the meadow, had probably noticed.

There was a small open truck at the edge of the road. He would only have to cross the meadow, passing between the prisoners and his men to reach it. Perhaps if he went to headquarters he would get some new order that this useless shooting, just as useless as the Italian officer's defiance, was to end.

It astonished him to have such a thought. How could he think such a thing when the enemy was there in front of him?

Tears of rage came to his eyes. Everyone was looking at him, Oberleutnant Karl Ritter, at his distraught face, his uncertainty and his sudden fear. It seemed as if Cefalonia, brilliant in the morning light now that the sun was high above the pine trees, had started to smoke.

He shut his eyes, but the bodies continued to fall in the darkness with the same vividness as they did in reality. He must go to headquarters to get rid of this sensation of nausea brought on by blood.

Was no one at headquarters or here amongst his soldiers aware that the sea had turned from blue to a mottled red colour, that blood was rising all round the island and beating on its shores?

At last, he made himself move and passed between the two opposing ranks.

For a moment he seemed to be walking on the brink of two worlds, poised between the world of the living and the world of the dead, and he felt that a gust of wind or a false step might force him into the world of the dead.

He stopped by the truck and wiped the sweat from his face with his hand. It was hot. The sun burned over the island and a heat haze, transparent and shimmering, rose from the sea and the mountains. Cefalonia was smoking.

But the sea had not lost its blue colour and the appearance of smoke was due only to the normal evaporation of water and the moisture in the earth.

He got into the truck and turned it towards Argostolion. He left the olive grove and the red villa with its bougainvillea-covered walls behind him. But by the bend the sound of machine gun fire reached him. His sergeant had taken his place. Would there be any more Italian officers left to execute or to save? he wondered without curiosity.

By the sea mills he met another convoy. The prisoners looked at him from the height of the trucks, their eyes, calm and questioning. Someone waved to him and then they were lost in the dust.

No, he would not get anything out of headquarters, he thought.

Then why was he making the effort? Perhaps those were the last lot from the division, and after all, had they not been beaten and were not they traitors?

On the doorstep, leaning against the doorpost, as though he was there by appointment, a vacant smile on his lips, stood Captain Puglisi. His jacket was unbuttoned and his shirt was open. On his tunic and shirt there were stains which in the darkness Katerina took to be sweat. She made him come in and shut the door.

The captain staggered and took a few uncertain steps across the floor. He groped for the edge of the table to support himself. From the way he stretched out his hands in front of him he seemed not to be able to see. Katerina was frightened and moved to help him, but he stood up by himself at the edge of the table. He remained there for a little in the light of the electric lamp, looking in front of him with sightless eyes.

'Captain,' said Katerina Pariotis. She had the impression that she was talking to someone a long way off, who was present only physically, whose mind was elsewhere. Then she understood that although he was still standing there and his heart was still beating beneath his bloodstained tunic and unbuttoned shirt, he was already dead.

With his face to the sun they had shot him against the wall of the Casetta Rossa along with the rest of the first load of officers.

'The sea, the sea, the sea,' he had thought confusedly when the German machine guns, little mouths of black metal, had started to fire. He had fallen to the ground and had felt a sensation of heat rise up into his mouth and the sour taste of hot metal and then of cloth and leather and then nothing. When he had reopened his eyes there was a strange silence. It was night and then there was shooting somewhere. All round there were bodies stretched out between the rocks and the aloes. Down there was a road. It was the road, the road to – he succeeded in remembering – to Argostolion, to Katerina's house, to the battery. He realized then that he too was lying there amidst the jackets and leather leggings of other officers, lying like this because – and he remembered again – because they had all been shot by Karl. By Karl Ritter.

His hands moved in front of him on the bare ground. They were clasping a tuft of grass. They stretched out towards a boot; they took hold of something; a cap. He was not dead then. He felt only a great thirst and a burning pain at the back of his neck; heat and thirst. That was odd, because it was night, a lovely starfilled night. The sea must have been somewhere near. He could hear its murmur singing in his ears, or perhaps it was blood.

A truck dark against the brightness of the metalled surface passed on the road from Argostolion. Its hooded headlights were two points of blue, hardly visible. It was filled with the silent shapes of more prisoners and German soldiers. Aldo Puglisi kept his hands still in front of him, because now he realized clearly that although he was not dead, they thought that he was dead. He must get to the house of Katerina Pariotis, because Katerina would help him. He must get to her climbing over this great barrier of uniforms, of bodies littered on the ground like empty sacks. Then he must follow the ditch along the road, avoiding the road itself so as not to get caught in the lights of a German vehicle or by a patrol. He pulled himself along, slowly, foot by foot, until finally he was opposite her gate. Only then did he cross the road. In the darkness of the garden he stopped for a moment to regain his breath, to pull himself together so as not to frighten little Katerina. She would help her captain, because she liked him a little. 'It is true, Katerina, it is true?' he had asked her.

Katerina had helped him to the room he had rented. He recognized the bed, the shaving mirror on the chest of drawers and the icon of Aghios Nicolaos above the bed. He recognized it all, and recognized the ceiling when Katerina and some other people, perhaps her mother and father – he did not succeed in seeing their faces through the mist of exhaustion and blood – helped to lay him on the bed.

He saw the pink painted ceiling with the lamp that hung down from it and the icon above his head.

'Katerina,' he said and then some other name which

Katerina could not catch. Was it his wife's name?

He uttered other words, but to Katerina who bent over him they were incomprehensible.

Then he closed his eyes and was silent.

4

Pasquale Lacerba had seen the long dark column of vehicles with their lights dimmed coming down the road to Capo San Teodoro. He had been in the middle of it seated on the floor of a German truck. He had seen the road grey in the night, smoothed by wheels and tracks, passing behind him beneath the radiator and between the wheels of the vehicle which followed. There had been an Italian driver at the wheel and a German soldier with his machine gun at the ready sitting on the wing watching him. Each vehicle had been the same, with one of the surviving drivers from the Italian division forced into the cabin to drive and the soldiers of Colonel Barge or Major von Hirchfeld sitting silent and weary in the back.

He had seen the sea the colour of ashes beyond the black mouths of the sea wells. There they had made him get down. Inside the wells the shapes of Italian soldiers and officers were piled up. He had been forced towards the sea almost having to dance to keep his balance on the rocks. He had got down into the wells to recover the shapes whilst above him glittered the barrel of a machine gun. Almost unexpectedly, when touched the shapes had acquired weight and consistency. They had become solid bodies. One by one he had hoisted them on his back, with their arms dangling in space. He had crossed the rocks slowly and carefully so as not to fall down with the corpses until he had learned to grope his way from the wells to the trucks and had been able to make the journey without looking.

He had seen the stars above the driver's cabin and the corpses heaped beside it. He had seen the tops of the trees on either side of the road and then suddenly he had stopped

183

as motionless as the stars. He had gone to work once more, but this time it was not the wells that he had had to attend to but long trenches cut in the earth beneath the pale olive trees. There one after another he had carried the corpses.

Then finally he had seen the light of the fires, kept going by the Germans with cans of petrol. Against the blaze they had seemed like puppets carved in wood, raising and lowering their arms in meaningless gestures, silent, without speaking. He had seen the barrel of a machine gun which had spat out at him, Pasquale Lacerba, former interpreter at divisional headquarters. He had seen a carpet of leaves upon which he had fallen, writhing, clutching at it with his hands; a cold vertical wall of leaves, become horizontal, on whose surface he had slipped and slid, towards a bottomless pit, with a searing pain here in his ankle towards which his hand had groped, a hand stained with blood.

5

No, it would not have been possible to recognize my father from those few bones enclosed in the box, and Padre Armao knew it. He remembered the white bones of dead soldiers. Greek public health workers had cleaned them of the earth which clung to them. In the presence of customs officials they had put them in paper sacks and then enclosed the sacks in little wooden boxes. On each box they had written a number. He remembered, one hundred, two hundred, two thousand. How many boxes had been numbered? He saw them again drawn up in so many rows laid out on the quayside, as though for a last parade, while they waited for the warship to come to carry them away.

He remembered the Italian chaplain, a survivor from the division, who had directed the work of exhumation. During that time he had travelled all over the island in an army lorry searching for the places where massacres had taken place, and the mass graves, and recovering bodies from the sea wells.

He was gathering together his children, as he had called them. He kept saying that all the dead had been like children to him. 'And now,' he had said, 'look, Padre Armao, look what has become of them: bones in paper sacks, sealed in little wooden boxes.'

CONCLUSION

CHAPTER TWENTY

NIGHT HAD FALLEN over Cefalonia. We had sat down at Nicolino's café, at a table on the pavement out in the open so that we could enjoy the warm air and the sights and sounds of Piazza Valianos. All the lights in the piazza were turned on, the old wrought iron lamp posts, the festoons of bulbs strung between them and in all the windows round the square, so that the rectangle of asphalt seemed as though it were lit up by the floodlights of a theatre. Down the middle of the square spattered with mud by the rain, there was a long crack dividing it into two irregular sections. Beneath the lights two semicircles of music stands, facing opposite sides of the piazza, had been set out in rows.

A crowd was gathering from the eucalyptus avenue and Via Principe Constantinos. Husbands and wives arm in arm holding children by the hand; young men and girls in separate groups, one behind the other, giggling and turning their heads to look behind them; old people coming more slowly, keeping apart from the main throng.

All around us the piazza was alive with sound. The tables inside the café as well as those on the pavement were taken. The little zinc trays laden with glasses rose and fell amongst the customers whose voices mingled with the laughter of the

187

passers by and the shouts of children playing amongst the flower beds.

Pasquale Lacerba greeted his friends. With his chin supported on the handle of his stick and his eyes shining in the light of the lamps, he followed the comings and goings of the townspeople attentively.

'Look at him,' he said to me under his breath, pointing his spectacles at the crowd, 'that little fellow, there, the well-dressed man with the flower in his buttonhole. He's the doctor.'

'Kalispera, Kalispera,' he cried, bowing slightly. And when the doctor had passed he turned towards me and said, 'He's got more horns on his head than hair'.

And then he said, 'You see that fine figure of a woman over there in the low cut dress showing all that bosom? Kalispera, Kyria, Kalispera,' he interrupted himself, bending over his stick.

'Well,' he went on in the same confidential and amused tone, 'well, she's the wife of a local lawyer. Don't ask me to elaborate. I'm a gentleman, I am. Don't make me say more.'

Round the corner from the seafront came the bonnet of a big bus. Its horn was blowing as it came into the piazza. The sound of voices grew louder and applause broke out. A group of girls swarmed out of its open door and gathered on the pavement. Some were carrying their instruments. Others waited at the side of the bus while the driver unloaded their instruments from the roof. A couple of boys wanting to impress the girls climbed up and laughing gave him a hand.

'The girls from Lixourion,' said Pasquale Lacerba. 'A fine looking lot and they play well; a bit odd, though, if you understand me.' He touched his forehead with a finger and staring at them through his glasses took a sip of ouzo.

I looked at the girls as they came down the pavement along the side of the piazza. They tripped along talking and laughing. Their eyes glittered like black stones. They wore white peaked caps on their heads with their hair falling down to their shoulders. Their bodices, embroidered with gold frogs, fitted tightly across their breasts. Their legs were firm and straight, crossing each other like a dancing forest.

What was odd about them, I asked. 'Oh,' said Pasquale Lacerba, 'it's just that they are from Lixourion.'

From the eucalyptus avenue burst the sound of a fanfare. The girls of Argostolion had awaited the arrival of the bus before making their entrance into the piazza. They came towards us in formation under the big trees in their green and yellow uniforms, with a blare of brass instruments, clashing of cymbals, and beat of drums. Their bare heads were held high, their breasts were thrust forward, as they moved a little stiffly in time with their rhythm. Their bare legs protruded from shorts. They reached the middle of the square, manoeuvring with the precision of an army drill squad.

'Ours,' said Pasquale Lacerba. 'You can see the difference, can't you; much more attractive. Look at their smart uniforms.' He took another sip. 'And their legs,' he added with a leer.

When they had reached the centre of the two semicircles of music stools the girls of Argostolion marked time, lifting their knees and stamping energetically on the ground with their heels. When the music stopped, they halted and stood to attention like soldiers. Applause broke out and cheers which echoed away beyond the light into the darkness of the town.

The girls from Lixourion took their places, too, but casually, without formality. They seemed a little subdued by the triumphal entry of their adversaries. The two bands arranged themselves one opposite the other beneath the lights which seemed to have grown in brightness, and spread out their music on the stands in front of their instruments.

The two conductors, who until this moment had kept out of sight, came into the piazza. Both of them were wearing ordinary clothes. They wore no ties and the collars of their shirts were open. They were both about the same height, small, insignificant looking men. They bowed politely to the applause that greeted them, and then turning their backs to each other rather as though they were going to fight a duel, they moved towards their bands. The conductor from Lixourion raised his baton, thin and trembling beneath the festoons of light. The girls took a deep breath and their bosoms swelled as they put their instruments to their lips. They breathed out and slow and solemn the introduction to *La Forza del Destino* filled the piazza, wafting like a soft wave over the café tables and the faces of the crowd who listened silently and attentively.

Pasquale Lacerba closed his eyes and beat time with his hand on the edge of the table. Taking up the opening theme, he hissed it between his teeth, accompanying it with movements of his head.

'They're not bad,' he said.

As the music gathered impetus, his hand beat out the rhythm more vigorously and the movement of his head became more marked and more precise. Seated at the little table, Pasquale Lacerba was conducting the orchestra, his face now serious and displeased at any shortcomings in the performance, now relaxed and happy.

People were sitting on benches in the piazza, others were listening standing up, watching the lights and their reflections in the brass instruments. I noticed Katerina Pariotis and the sea captain seated at a table on the pavement opposite us across the square. She was eating an ice from a goblet. Every now and again she paused with her spoon in mid-air as though the better to hear something. The old sailor was sipping a glass of yellow wine and his movements suggested that he, too, was listening.

It was an evening perfect of its kind. The air was soft and there were the stars and the sea and the girls from the two towns in their gay uniforms, and there was Pasquale Lacerba, the orchestral conductor. On the far side of the piazza Sandrino was sitting on the wing of his taxi, his arms folded. He too, was completely lost in listening.

Argostolion, on such an evening, was quite different from the dead place of my arrival, from the squalid town that I had seen that morning. The whole island had changed, and the bay breathing peacefully out there beyond the last building was changed too.

And yet, I thought, a few miles from Argostolion was the

Casetta Rossa. The Italian cemetery was there, too, and the sea wells and the ditches. Everywhere there were memories and reminders of a massacre that not even the earthquake had been able to blot out. The threat of an earthquake was always there. How was it possible to forget even for one evening that death lay hidden and brooding in Cefalonia's heart?

Was it possible to get so used to death that in the end one did not notice it? The introduction had come to an end amidst a thunder of applause. Even Pasquale Lacerba clapped and smiled.

'Splendid girls, splendid, even though they do come from Lixourion,' he said. 'But now you will hear ours. In a different class altogether, my friend, a different class. We Italians understand these things. We've an ear for them. You'll see . . .'

And as the band of Argostolion threw themselves with vigour into the opening bars of the overture to *William Tell,* Pasquale Lacerba closed his eyes once more and gave himself up to his game of conducting an orchestra.

They were better than the others. I could tell from his smile and from the smiles and increased attention of the rest of the crowd.

Yes, it was possible. It was even right that it should be so, I told myself as I looked at the unknown faces around us. From birth onwards each one of us carries death around with him, and we get so used to it that we do not notice it. It was right, I repeated, that life and death should be confused together, cancelling out the significance and memory of each other.

Just as was happening this evening before my eyes here on Cefalonia.

'Listen, listen to this passage,' whispered Pasquale Lacerba, and his bony, sunburnt hand continued to beat time. His eyes were closed and on his face there was a look of bliss.